A Hatful of Seuss

RANDOM HOUSE
NEW YORK

This compilation was originally published in 1996 by Random House Children's Books, a division of Random House, Inc.

Published in the United States by Random House Children's Books, a division of Random House, Inc., New York.

RANDOM HOUSE and colophon are registered trademarks of Random House, Inc.

www.randomhouse.com/kids
www.seussville.com

Educators and librarians, for a variety of teaching tools, visit us at www.randomhouse.com/teachers

Library of Congress Cataloging-in-Publication Data
Seuss, Dr.
A hatful of Seuss : by Dr. Seuss.
p. cm.
SUMMARY: A compilation of five works of Dr. Seuss, including "Bartholomew and the Oobleck," "If I Ran the Zoo," "The Sneetches and Other Stories," "Dr. Seuss's Sleep Book," and "Horton Hears a Who!"
ISBN: 978-0-679-88388-3 (trade)
1. Humorous stories, American. 2. Children's stories, American.
[1. Humorous stories. 2. Stories in rhyme. 3. Short stories.]
I. Title.
PZ8.3.G27Hat 1997 [E]—dc20 96-25038

Printed in the United States of America 22 21 20 19 18 17 16 15 14 13

Contents

A Hatful of Seuss

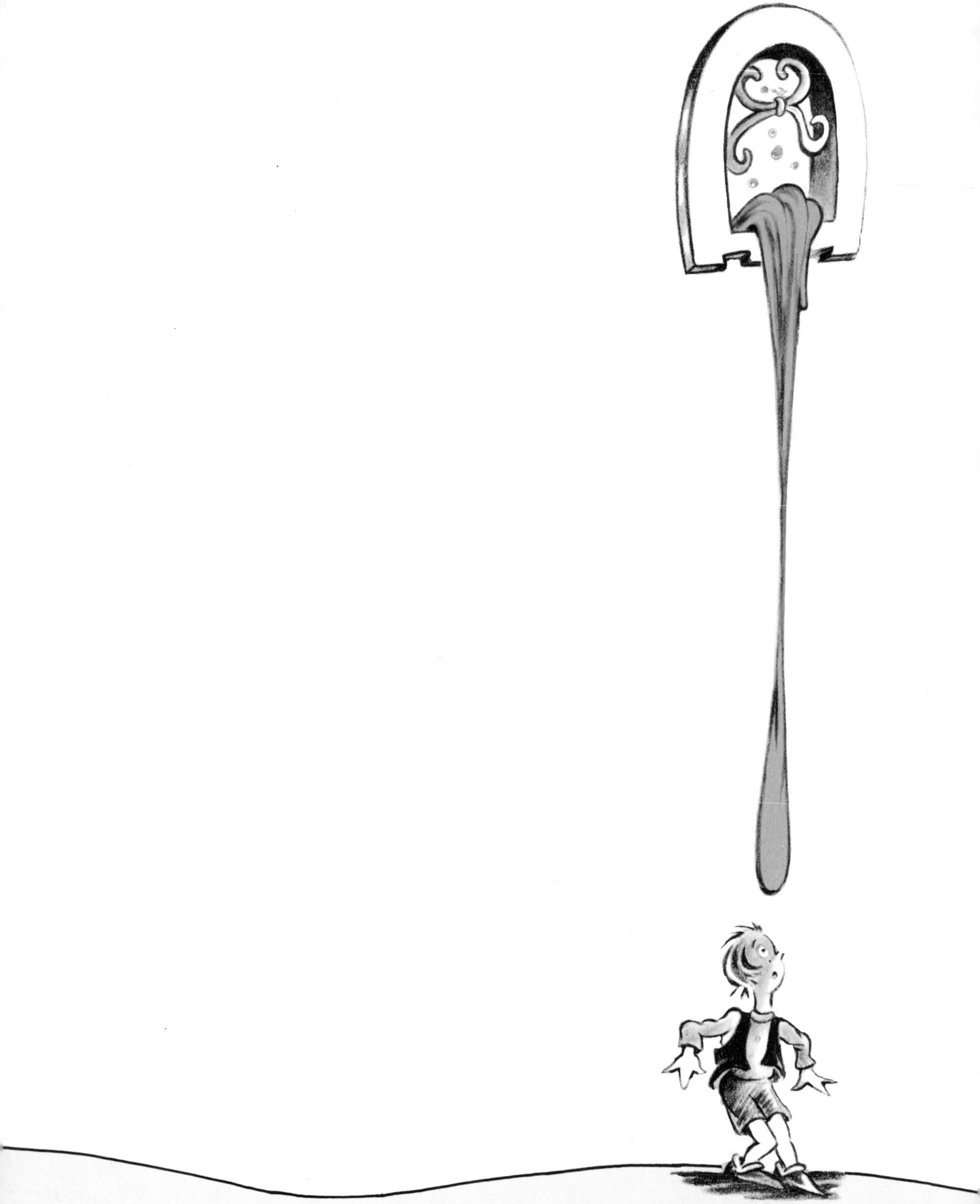

BARTHOLOMEW and the OOBLECK

THEY still talk about it in the Kingdom of Didd as The-Year-the-King-Got-Angry-with-the-Sky. And they still talk about the page boy, Bartholomew Cubbins. If it hadn't been for Bartholomew Cubbins, that King and that Sky would have wrecked that little Kingdom.

Bartholomew had seen the King get angry many, many times before. But *that* year when His Majesty started growling at the *sky,* Bartholomew Cubbins just didn't know what to make of it.

Yet all that year, the old King did it. All year long he stared up into the air above his kingdom, muttering and sputtering through his royal whiskers, "Humph! The things that come down from my sky!"

All spring when the rain came down, he growled at *that* . . .

All summer when the sunshine came down, he growled at *that* . . .

All autumn when the fog came down,

he growled at *that* . . .

And that winter when the snow came down, he started shouting! "This snow! This fog! This sunshine! This rain! BAHH! These four things that come down from my sky!"

"But, King Derwin," Bartholomew tried to calm him. "You've *always* had these same four things come down."

"That's just the trouble!" bellowed the King. "Every year the *same* four things! I'm mighty tired of those old things! I want something NEW to come down!"

"Something *new* come down . . . ?" Bartholomew gasped. "That's impossible, Your Majesty. You just can't have it."

"Boy, don't you dare tell me what I can or cannot have! Remember, Bartholomew, I am King!"

"I know, Sire," said Bartholomew. "You rule all the land. And you rule all the people. But even kings can't rule the *sky*."

"Can't, eh?" His Majesty flew into a terrible rage. "Well, maybe *other* kings can't do it, but maybe I'm one king who can! You mark my words, Bartholomew Cubbins, I *will* have something new come down!"

But *how* to get something new to come down . . . ? That was rather hard to think up. And for many days the old King stomped around, trying to figure out *some* way to do it.

Then, finally, late one night, when all the lords and ladies of the palace were fast asleep . . . just as the King was buttoning his royal nightshirt . . . he suddenly stopped still. A strange wild light began to shine in his gray-green eyes.

"Why, of course!" He began laughing. "*They* can do it for me! Bartholomew Cubbins, blow my secret whistle! Quick! Call my royal magicians!"

"Your *magicians,* Your Majesty?" Bartholomew shivered. "Oh, no, Your Majesty! Don't call *them!*"

"You hold your tongue, Bartholomew Cubbins! You do as I command you. Blow my secret whistle!"

"Yes, Sire," Bartholomew bowed. "But, Your Majesty, I still think that you may be very sorry."

He took the King's secret whistle from its secret hook. He blew a long, low blast down the King's back secret stairway.

And a moment later he heard them coming! Up from their musty hole beneath the dungeon, up the empty midnight tunnel to the royal bedchamber tower, came the magicians on their padded, shuffling feet. Up and right into the room they came chanting:

"Shuffle, duffle, muzzle, muff.
Fista, wista, mista-cuff.
We are men of groans and howls,
Mystic men who eat boiled owls.
Tell us what you wish, oh King.
Our magic can do anything."

"I wish," spoke the King, "to have you make something fall from my skies that no other kingdom has ever had before. What can you do? What will you make?"

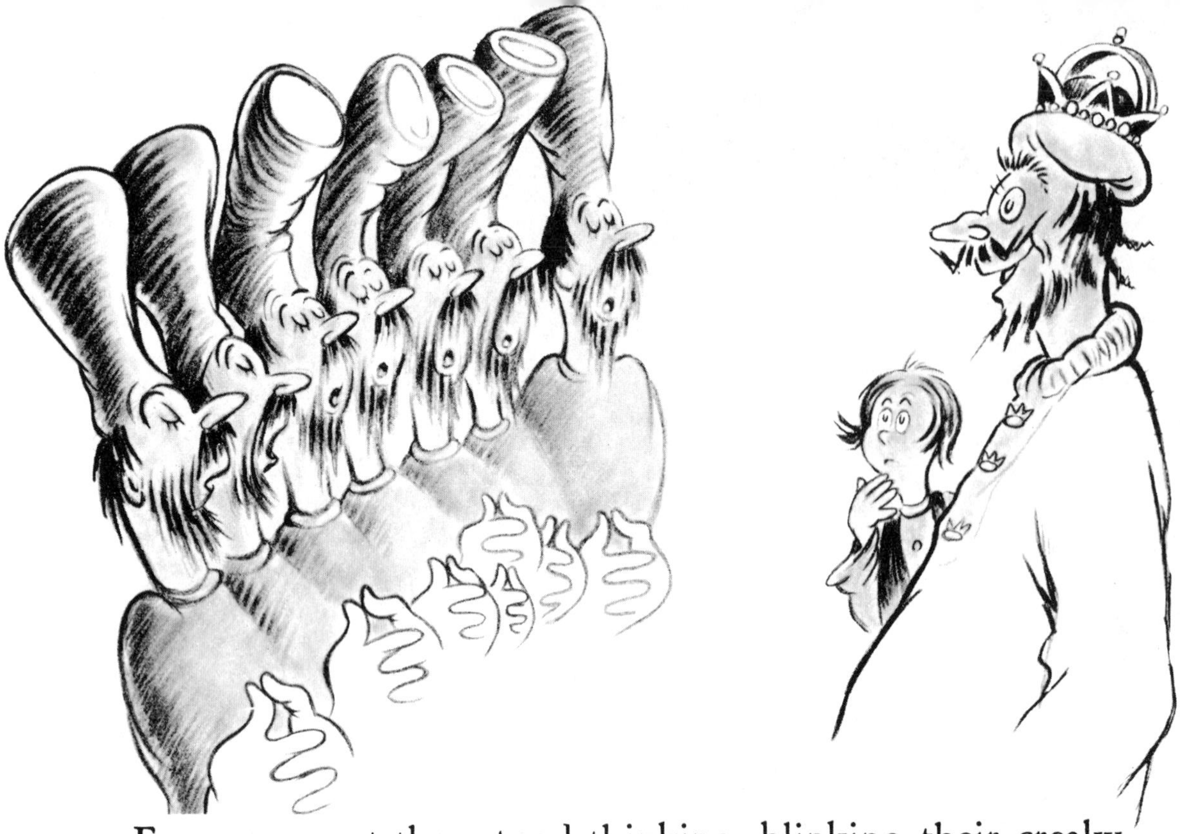

For a moment they stood thinking, blinking their creaky eyes. Then they spoke a word . . . one word . . . "Oobleck."

"Oobleck . . . ?" asked the King. "What will it look like?"

"Won't look like rain. Won't look like snow.
Won't look like fog. That's all we know.
We just can't tell you any more.
We've never made oobleck before."

They bowed. They started toward the door.

"We go now to our secret cave
On Mystic Mountain Neeka-tave.
There, all night long, we'll work for you
And you'll have oobleck when we're through!"

"They'll do something crazy!" whispered Bartholomew. "Call them back, Your Majesty! Stop them!"

"Stop them? Not for a ton of diamonds!" chuckled the King. "Why, I'll be the mightiest man that ever lived! Just think of it! Tomorrow I'm going to have OOBLECK!"

It took Bartholomew a long time to get the excited King to sleep that night. But there was no sleep for Bartholomew, the page boy. All night long he stood in the King's window, staring out at the Mystic Mountain Neeka-tave. Somewhere up there, Bartholomew knew, the magicians were working their terrible magic.

All night the magicians did. All night they walked circles round their magic fire, making magic mumbling with their clucking tongues:

"Oh, snow and rain are not enough!
Oh, we must make some brand-new stuff!
So feed the fire with wet mouse hair,
Burn an onion. Burn a chair.
Burn a whisker from your chin
And burn a long sour lizard skin.
Burn yellow twigs and burn red rust
And burn a stocking full of dust.
Make magic smoke, green, thick and hot!
(It sure smells dreadful, does it not?)
That means the smoke is now just right
So, quick! Before the day gets light,
Go, magic smoke! Go high! Go high!
Go rise into the kingdom's sky!
Go make the oobleck tumble down
On every street, in every town!
Go make the wondrous oobleck fall!
Oh, bring down oobleck on us all!"

Dawn was just breaking and Bartholomew was still standing . . . trembling, watching at the bedchamber window. But now, as the sun rose, Bartholomew smiled. Those silly magicians hadn't done a thing!

Then, suddenly, Bartholomew Cubbins stopped smiling.

Was he seeing things . . . ? No! There *was* something strange up there in the sky!

At first it seemed like a little greenish cloud . . . just a wisp of greenish steam. But now it was coming lower, closer, down toward the fields and farms and houses of the sleeping little kingdom.

It was swirling around the topmost turrets of the palace. Tiny little greenish specks were shimmering in the air right

over his head. Queer little greenish blobs, just about the size of grape seeds!

He stretched out his hand. He started to catch one. Then he pulled his hand back! There was something frightening about those blobs. Bartholomew slammed the window shut.

"Wake up, Your Majesty!" he shouted. "Your oobleck! It's falling!"

The King sprang out of his royal bed sheets.

"By my royal whiskers, it is!" he cried. "Oh, that beautiful oobleck! And it's mine! All mine!"

"I don't like the looks of those blobs, Sire," said Bartholomew. "They're coming down now as big as greenish peanuts."

"The bigger the better!" laughed the King. "Oh, what a day! I'm going to make it a holiday! I want every man, woman and child in my kingdom to go out and dance in my glorious oobleck!"

"Out in *that* stuff . . . ?" asked Bartholomew. "Do you really think it's safe, Sire?"

"Stop asking foolish questions!" snapped the King. "Boy, you run to my royal bell tower. Wake my royal bell ringer. Tell him to ring the great holiday bell!"

For a moment Bartholomew Cubbins didn't move.

"Run!" barked the King. Bartholomew ran.

Across the sleeping palace, Bartholomew ran. Then up the ladder of the high bell tower, he climbed to the bell ringer's little cubbyhole in the belfry.

"Ring your bell!" he called. "His Majesty the King proclaims today a holiday!"

The old man crawled out of his cot. He grabbed the bell rope. "What's the holiday for, Bartholomew?"

"You'll find out soon enough!" said Bartholomew.

The bell ringer yanked the rope. Nothing happened.

He yanked it harder. Still nothing happened.

"Heh . . . ? What's wrong with my bell?" he murmured. "I'd better take a look outside."

He poked his head out through the little trap door.

"Merciful gracious!" he gulped. "What is THAT? All over my bell like greenish molasses!"

"Not only your bell!" Bartholomew cried. "Look at that poor robin down there in that tree! She's stuck to her nest! She can't move a wing! That oobleck's gooey! It's gummy! It's like glue!"

"Oooh!" The bell ringer wrung his hands. "If that green stuff sticks up *robins,* it'll stick up *people,* too!"

"Someone's got to warn the people!" cried Bartholomew. "Got to wake 'em and warn 'em to stay inside their houses! I'll tell the royal trumpeter!" he shouted. He turned and slid like lightning down the bell tower ladder.

To the trumpeter's tower raced Bartholomew Cubbins, and on up the steps four stairs at a time.

As he ran he could hear the *"Plop! Plop!"* of the oobleck on the windowpanes. It was pelting against the palace walls as big as greenish cup-cakes now!

He yanked the covers off the snoring trumpeter. He shoved his cold trumpet right into his sleepy hands.

"Get up! Warn the people! Blow the alarm!"

"Alarm . . . ?" yawned the trumpeter. Then his eyes saw the oobleck. "Those green things, Bartholomew! Where'd *they* come from?"

"The King . . ." panted Bartholomew. "His royal magicians made them!"

The royal trumpeter leapt from his bed. "That King of ours should be ashamed!" He jabbed his trumpet out of the window. "I'll blow," he shouted, "the loudest alarm that's ever been heard in the Kingdom of Didd!"

But all the royal trumpeter blew was a "GLUGG!"

"My horn!" he gulped. "One of those green things flew inside it!"

He tried to blow it out. He couldn't blow it out.

He tried to shake it out. He couldn't shake it out.

"I'll get it *somehow!*" he yelled. "I'll *pull* it out!"

"No!" shouted Bartholomew. "Don't you touch it!"

The trumpeter's hand was already in it. His fingers grabbed hold of the lump of oobleck. He could feel it squiggle around in his fist like a slippery potato dumpling made of rubber.

He pulled with all his might. The oobleck began to stretch. Then, *"Gloing!"* the oobleck snapped back inside the trumpet. It yanked his arm back with it right up to the elbow.

"I can't wiggle a finger!" the trumpeter wailed. "Oh, Bartholomew, what'll I do?"

"I don't know. And I hate to leave you stuck to your horn. But if *you* can't warn the people of the kingdom, I've got to find someone who can!"

Out of the room and down the stairs raced Bartholomew Cubbins . . .

. . . down to the chamber of the Captain of the Guards. The Captain was humming in front of his mirror, combing the ends of his handsome moustache.

"Captain! DO something!" shouted Bartholomew.

"Do something? Why?" smiled the Captain. "What's wrong?"

"Captain! Haven't you seen the dreadful oobleck? It's coming down now as big as greenish baseballs!"

"Oh, *that* stuff," laughed the Captain. "What's so dreadful about that, lad? You know, *I* think it's rather pretty."

"Captain!" pleaded Bartholomew. "It's dangerous!"

"Nonsense!" snorted the Captain. "Lad, are you trying to frighten *me*? Captains, my boy, are afraid of nothing. That stuff's harmless. I'll show you. I'll eat some."

"Eat some . . . ?" gasped Bartholomew. "Oh, *no!"*

But before Bartholomew could stop him, the Captain was leaning out his window, scooping up some oobleck on the end of his sword.

"Don't, Captain! DON'T!"

The Captain did! By the time Bartholomew dragged him back inside the room, his mouth was glued tight shut with oobleck. He tried to speak, but no words came out. All the noble Captain of the Guards could do was blow a lot of little sticky greenish bubbles.

"Forgive me for leaving you, Captain," said Bartholomew. "But a captain full of bubbles is no help at all." Bartholomew stretched the poor man out. He left him there on his chamber floor.

Bartholomew went tearing through the zigzag palace hallways. "I'll get the King's horse! I'll ride through the country! I'll warn the people of the kingdom myself!"

He pushed open the door that led out to the Royal Stables.

Bartholomew stopped. He could go no farther. The awful oobleck was plumping down as big as greenish footballs now!

Too late to warn the people of the kingdom! There were farmers in the fields, getting stuck to hoes and plows. Goats were getting stuck to ducks. Geese were getting stuck to cows.

Outside the palace it was piling up, great greenish tons of oobleck, deeper and deeper on every roof in the land.

There was nothing Bartholomew Cubbins could do out there. Shaking his head sadly, he stepped back inside.

But inside, a moment later, it was just as bad as out!

With an angry roar, the oobleck was suddenly hitting the palace harder. It was battering and spattering against the walls as big as greenish buckets full of gooey asparagus soup!

Like a sinking sailboat, the whole palace was springing leaks. The oobleck was ripping the windows right off their hinges.

It was dripping through the ceilings. It was rolling down the chimneys. It was coming in everywhere . . . even through the keyholes!

From every bedroom in the palace came the howls of lords and ladies. Frightened, in their nightgowns, they came jumping to their doors.

"Go back to your beds! Get under your blankets!" Bartholomew Cubbins went crying through the halls.

But nobody paid the slightest attention. Everyone in the palace started rushing madly about.

The Royal Cook rushed down to the royal kitchen. Bartholomew Cubbins saw him trapped there, stuck to three stew pots, a tea cup and a cat!

The Royal Laundress rushed outside to save her laundry. Bartholomew saw her, stuck tight to the clothesline, between two woolen stockings and the King's best Sunday blouse!

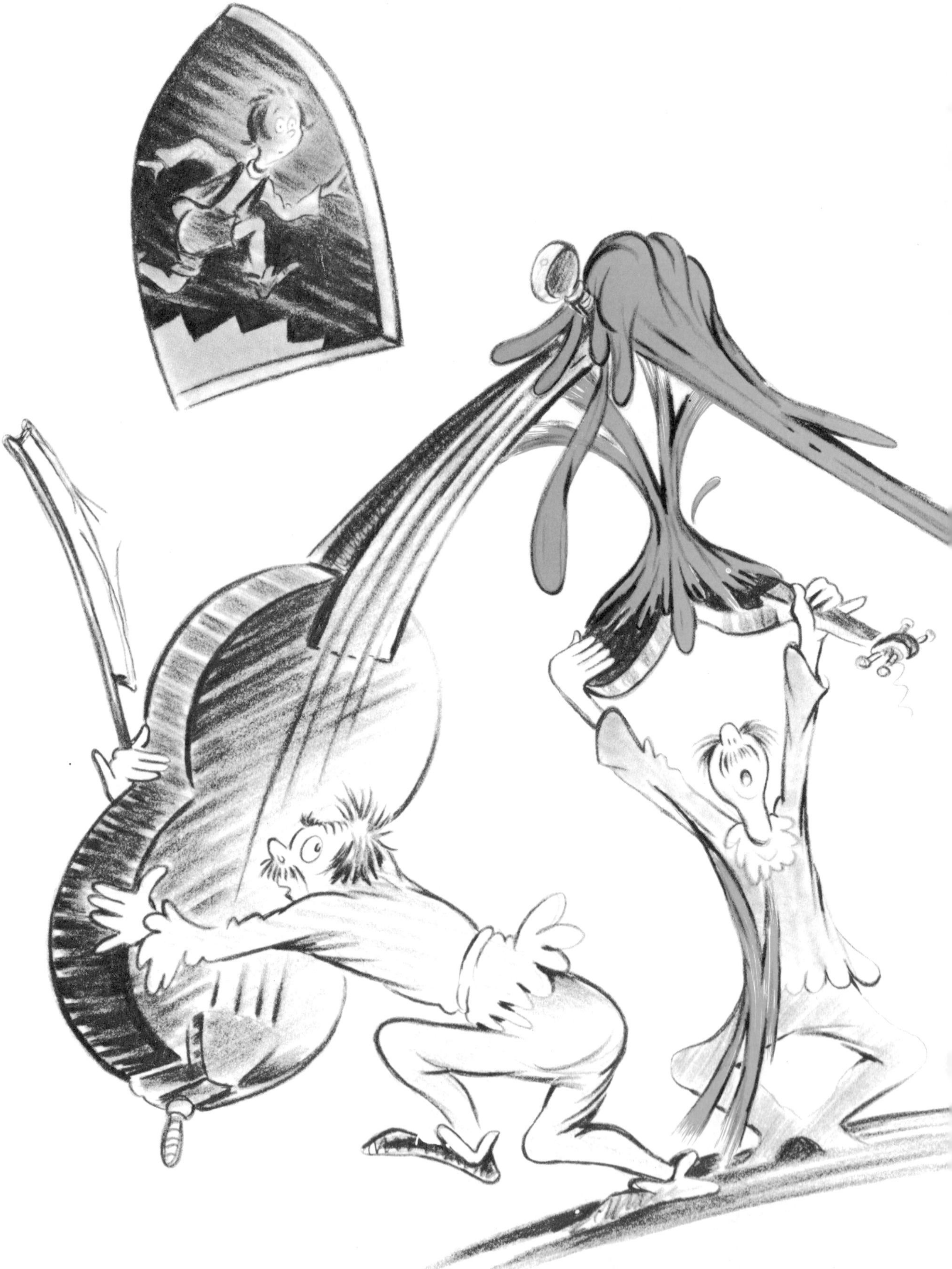

He saw the Royal Fiddlers. They were stuck to their royal fiddles! Everywhere Bartholomew ran, he saw someone stuck to something!

They were stuck up by the dozens! Every last friend he had in the world was flopping and floundering, all hopelessly caught in the goo.

Then, suddenly midst the hubbub, Bartholomew gasped, *"The King!"* Where *was* the King? He'd forgotten all about him!

It was in the throne room that Bartholomew found him.

There he sat . . . Old King Derwin, proud and mighty ruler of the Kingdom of Didd, trembling, shaking, helpless as a baby.

His royal crown was stuck to his royal head. The seat of his royal pants were stuck to his royal throne. Oobleck was dripping from his royal eyebrows. It was oozing into his royal ears.

"Fetch my magicians, Bartholomew!" he commanded. "Make them say some magic words! Make them stop the oobleck falling!"

Bartholomew shrugged his shoulders. "I can't fetch them, Your Majesty. Their cave on Mountain Neeka-tave is buried deep in oobleck."

"Then *I* must think of some magic words!" groaned the King. "Oh, what are those words my magicians say . . . ? *Shuffle . . . duffle . . . muzzle . . . muff* . . . That's all I can remember and they don't do any good! The oobleck keeps on falling harder!"

Bartholomew Cubbins could hold his tongue no longer.

"And it's going to keep on falling," he shouted, "until your whole great marble palace tumbles down! So don't waste your time saying foolish *magic* words. YOU ought to be saying some plain *simple* words!"

"*Simple* words . . . ? What do you mean, boy?"

"I mean," said Bartholomew, "this is all *your* fault! Now, the least you can do is say the simple words, 'I'm sorry'."

No one had ever talked to the King like this before.

"What!" he bellowed. "ME . . . *ME* say I'm sorry! Kings *never* say 'I'm sorry!' And I am the mightiest king in all the world!"

Bartholomew looked the King square in the eye.

"You may be a mighty king," he said. "But you're sitting in oobleck up to your chin. And so is everyone else in your land. And if you won't even say you're sorry, *you're no sort of a king at all!*"

Bartholomew Cubbins turned his back. He started for the throne room door.

But then Bartholomew heard a great, deep sob. The old King was crying! "Come back, Bartholomew Cubbins! You're right! It *is* all my fault! And I *am* sorry! Oh, Bartholomew, I'm awfully, *awfully* sorry!"

And the moment the King spoke those words, something happened . . .

Maybe there *was* something magic in those simple words, "I'm sorry."

Maybe there *was* something magic in those simple words, "It's all my fault."

Maybe there was, and maybe there wasn't. But they say that as soon as the old King spoke them, the sun began to shine and fight its way through the storm. They say that the falling oobleck blobs grew smaller and smaller and smaller.

They say that all the oobleck that was stuck on all the people and on all the animals of the Kingdom of Didd just simply, quietly melted away.

And then, they say, Bartholomew took the old King by the sleeve . . .

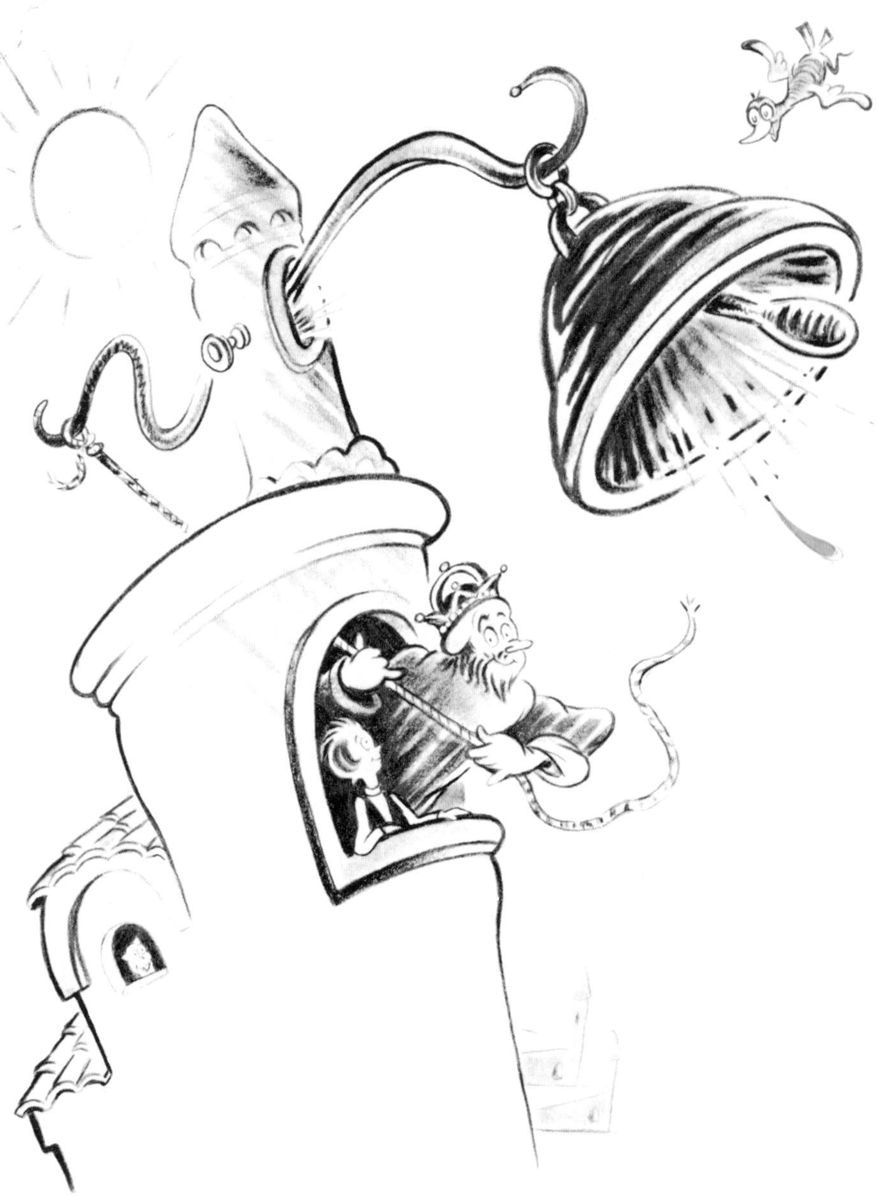

. . . and led him up the steps of the high bell tower. He put the bell rope into His Majesty's royal hands and the King himself rang the holiday bell.

Then the King proclaimed a brand-new national holiday . . . in honor of the four perfect things that come down from the sky.

The King now knew that these four old-fashioned things . . . the rain, the sunshine, the fog and the snow . . . were good enough for any king in all the world, especially for him, old King Derwin of Didd.

IF I RAN The ZOO

"It's a pretty good zoo,"
Said young Gerald McGrew,
"And the fellow who runs it
Seems proud of it, too."

"But if *I* ran the zoo,"
Said young Gerald McGrew,
"I'd make a few changes.
That's just what I'd do . . ."

The lions and tigers and that kind of stuff
They have up here now are not *quite* good enough.
You see things like these in just any old zoo.
They're awfully old-fashioned. I want something *new!*

So I'd open each cage. I'd unlock every pen,
Let the animals go, and start over again.
And, somehow or other, I think I could find
Some beasts of a much more un-usual kind.

ZOO

A *four*-footed lion's not much of a beast.
The one in my zoo will have *ten* feet, at least!
Five legs on the left and five more on the right.
Then people will stare and they'll say, "What a sight!
This Zoo Keeper, New Keeper Gerald's quite keen.
That's the gol-darndest lion I ever have seen!"

ZOO

My New Zoo, McGrew Zoo, will make people talk.
My New Zoo, McGrew Zoo, will make people gawk
At the strangest odd creatures that ever did walk.
I'll get, for my zoo, a new sort-of-a-hen
Who roosts in another hen's topknot, and *then*
Another one roosts in the topknot of his,
And another in *his,* and another in HIS,
And so forth and upward and onward, gee whizz!

But that's just a start. I'll do better than *that*.
They'll see me next day, in my zoo-keeper's hat,
Coming into my zoo with an Elephant-Cat!

They'll be so surprised they'll all swallow their gum.
They'll ask, when they see my strange animals come,
"Where *do* you suppose he gets things like that from?
His animals all have such very odd faces.
I'll bet he must hunt them in rather odd places!"

And that's what I'll do,
Said young Gerald McGrew.
If you want to catch beasts you don't see every day,
You have to go places quite out-of-the-way.
You have to go places no others can get to.
You have to get cold and you have to get wet, too.
Up past the North Pole, where the frozen winds squeal,
I'll go and I'll hunt in my Skeegle-mobile
And bring back a family of *What-do-you-know!*
And that's how my New Zoo, McGrew Zoo, will grow.

ZOO

I'll hunt in the mountains of Zomba-ma-Tant
With helpers who all wear their eyes at a slant,
And capture a fine fluffy bird called the Bustard
Who only eats custard with sauce made of mustard.
And, also, a very fine beast called the Flustard
Who only eats mustard with sauce made of custard.

ZOO

I'll catch 'em in caves and I'll catch 'em in brooks,
I'll catch 'em in crannies, I'll catch 'em in nooks
That you don't read about in geography books.

I'll catch 'em in countries that no one can spell
Like the country of Motta-fa-Potta-fa-Pell.
In a country like that, if a hunter is clever,
He'll hunt up some beasts that you never saw ever!

I'll load up five boats with a family of Joats
Whose feet are like cows', but wear squirrel-skin coats
And sit down like dogs, but have voices like goats –
Excepting they can't sing the very high notes.

McG.

And then I'll go down to the Wilds of Nantucket
And capture a family of Lunks in a bucket.
Then people will say, "Now I like that boy heaps.
His New Zoo, McGrew Zoo, is growing by leaps.
He captures them wild and he captures them meek,
He captures them slim and he captures them sleek.
What *do* you suppose he will capture next week?"

I'll capture one tiny. I'll capture one cute.
I'll capture a deer that no hunter would shoot.
A deer that's so nice he could sleep in your bed
If it weren't for those horns that he has on his head.

CITY
ZOO
G. McGREW, MANAGER
ZOO

And speaking of horns that are just a bit queer,
I'll bring back a very odd family of deer:
A father, a mother, two sisters, a brother
Whose horns are connected, from one to the other,
Whose horns are so mixed they can't tell them apart,
Can't tell where they end and can't tell where they start!
Each deer's mighty puzzled. He's never yet found
If *his* horns are *hers,* or the other way 'round.

I'll capture them fat and I'll capture them scrawny.
I'll capture a scraggle-foot Mulligatawny,
A high-stepping animal fast as the wind
From the blistering sands of the Desert of Zind.
This beast is the beast that the brave chieftains ride
When they want to go fast to find some place to hide.
A Mulligatawny is fine for my zoo
And so is a chieftain. I'll bring one back, too.

In the Far Western part
Of south-east North Dakota
Lives a very fine animal
Called the Iota.
But I'll capture one
Who is even much finer
In the north-eastern west part
Of South Carolina.

When people see *him,* they will say, "Now, by thunder!
This New Zoo, McGrew Zoo, is really a wonder!"

Most beasts are quite friendly, but still, in some lands
Some beasts are too dangerous to catch with bare hands.
For those that are ugly and vicious and mean
I'll build a Bad-Animal-Catching-Machine.
It's rather expensive to build such a kit,
But with it a hunter can never get bit.

A zoo should have bugs, so I'll capture a Thwerll
Whose legs are snarled up in a terrible snerl.

And then I'll go out and I'll capture some Chuggs,
Some keen-shooter, mean-shooter, bean-shooter bugs.

I'll go to the African island of Yerka
And bring back a tizzle-topped Tufted Mazurka,
A kind of canary with quite a tall throat.
His neck is so long, if he swallows an oat
For breakfast the first day of April, they say
It has to go down such a very long way
That it gets to his stomach the fifteenth of May.

I'll bag a big bug
Who is very surprising,
A feller who has
A propeller for rising
And zooming around
Making cross-country hops,
From Texas to Boston
With only two stops.
Now *that* sort of thing
For a bug is just tops!

And when I've caught *him,*
Then the next thing you know
I'll go and I'll capture
A wild Tick-Tack-Toe,
With X's that win
And with Zeros that lose.
He'll look mighty good
In this Zoo of McGrew's.

I'll bring back a Gusset, a Gherkin, a Gasket
And also a Gootch from the wilds of Nantasket.

And eight Persian Princes will carry the basket,
But what *their* names are, I don't know. So don't ask it.

In a cave in Kartoom lives a beast called the Natch
That no other hunter's been able to catch.
He's hidden for years in his cave with a pout
And no one's been able to make him come out.
But *I'll* coax him out with a wonderful meal
That's cooked by my cooks in my Cooker-mobile.

They'll fix up a dish that is just to his taste;
Three chicken croquettes made of library paste,
Then sprinkled with peanut shucks, pickled and spiced,
Then baked at 600 degrees and then iced.
It's mighty hard cooking to cook up such feasts
But that's how the New Zoo, McGrew Zoo, gets beasts.

I'll go to the far-away Mountains of Tobsk
Near the River of Nobsk, and I'll bring back an Obsk,
A sort of a kind of a Thing-a-ma-Bobsk
Who only eats rhubarb and corn-on-the-cobsk.
Then people will flock to my zoo in a mobsk.
"McGrew," they will say, "does a wonderful jobsk!
He hunts with such vim and he hunts with such vigor,
His New Zoo, McGrew Zoo, gets bigger and bigger!"

OBSK

And, speaking of birds, there's the Russian Palooski,
Whose headski is redski and belly is blueski.
I'll get one of *them* for my Zooski McGrewski.

Then the whole town will gasp, "Why, this boy never sleeps!
No keeper before ever kept what *he* keeps!
There's no telling WHAT that young fellow will do!"
And then, just to show them, I'll sail to Ka-Troo

And

Bring

Back

a NERKLE
a NERD
and a SEERSUCKER, too!

ZOO

I'll hunt in the Jungles of Hippo-no-Hungus
And bring back a flock of wild Bippo-no-Bungus!
The Bippo-no-Bungus from Hippo-no-Hungus
Are better than those down in Dippo-no-Dungus
And smarter than those out in Nippo-no-Nungus.
And that's why I'll catch 'em in Hippo-no-Hungus
Instead of those others in Nungus and Dungus.
And people will say when they see these Bips bounding,
"This Zoo Keeper, New Keeper's simply astounding!
He travels so far that you'd think he would drop!
When *do* you suppose this young fellow will stop?"

Stop . . . ?
Well, I should.
But I won't stop until
I've captured the Fizza-ma-Wizza-ma-Dill,
The world's biggest bird from the Island of Gwark
Who only eats pine trees and spits out the bark.
And boy! When I get *him* back home to my park,
The whole *world* will say, "Young McGrew's made his mark.
He's built a zoo better than Noah's whole Ark!
These wonderful, marvelous beasts that he chooses
Have made him the greatest of all the McGrewses!"

McGREW'S
ZOO!
ENTRANCE

"WOW!" They'll all cheer,
"What this zoo must be worth!
It's the gol-darndest zoo
On the face of the earth!"

"Yes . . .
That's what I'd do,"
Said young Gerald McGrew.
"I'd make a few changes
If *I* ran the zoo."

HORTON HEARS A WHO!

On the fifteenth of May, in the Jungle of Nool,
In the heat of the day, in the cool of the pool,
He was splashing . . . enjoying the jungle's great joys . . .
When Horton the elephant heard a small noise.

So Horton stopped splashing. He looked toward the sound.
"That's funny," thought Horton. "There's no one around."
Then he heard it again! Just a very faint yelp
As if some tiny person were calling for help.
"I'll help you," said Horton. "But *who* are you? *Where?*"
He looked and he looked. He could see nothing there
But a small speck of dust blowing past through the air.

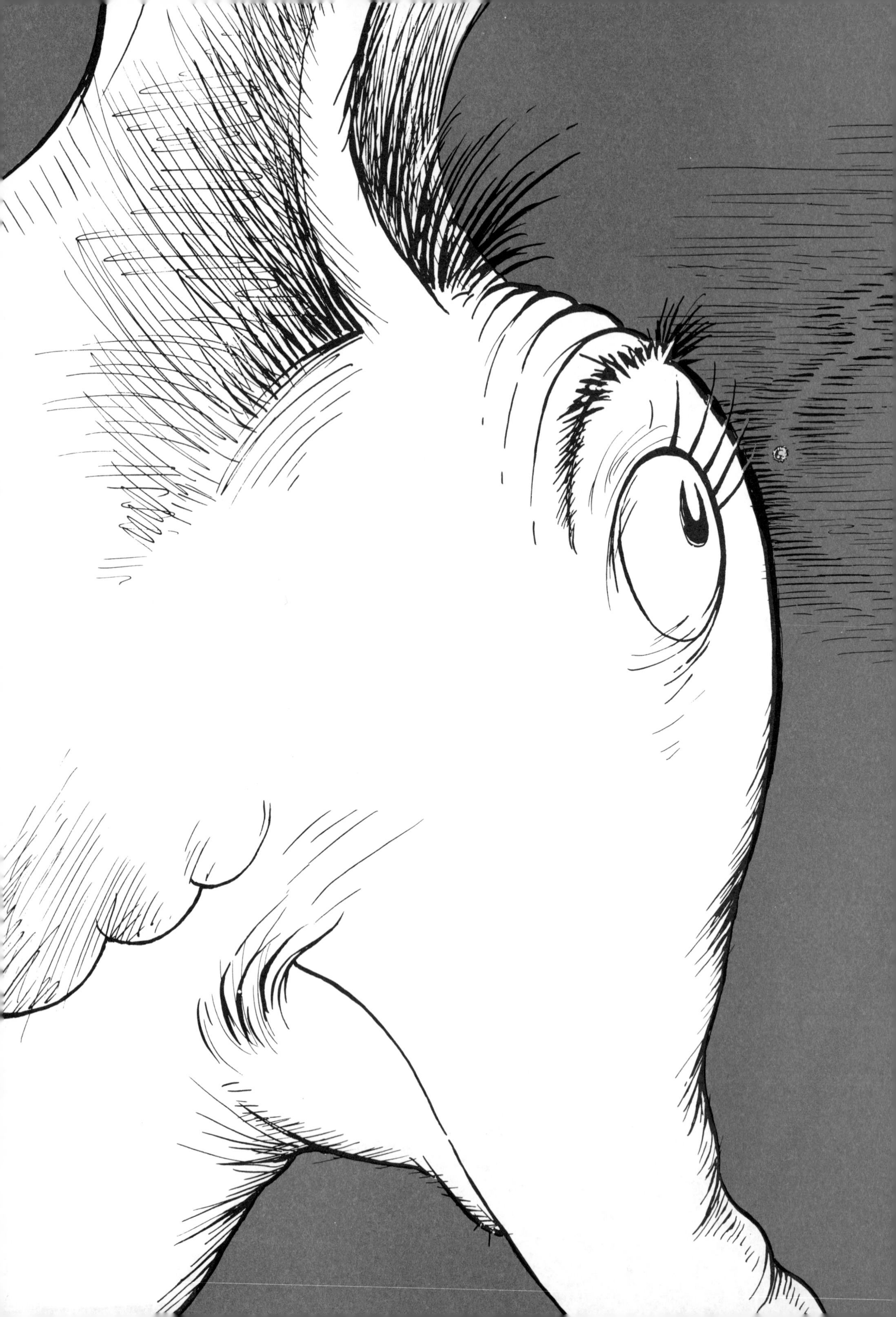

"I say!" murmured Horton. "I've never heard tell
Of a small speck of dust that is able to yell.
So you know what I think? . . . Why, I think that there must
Be someone on top of that small speck of dust!
Some sort of a creature of *very* small size,
Too small to be seen by an elephant's eyes. . .

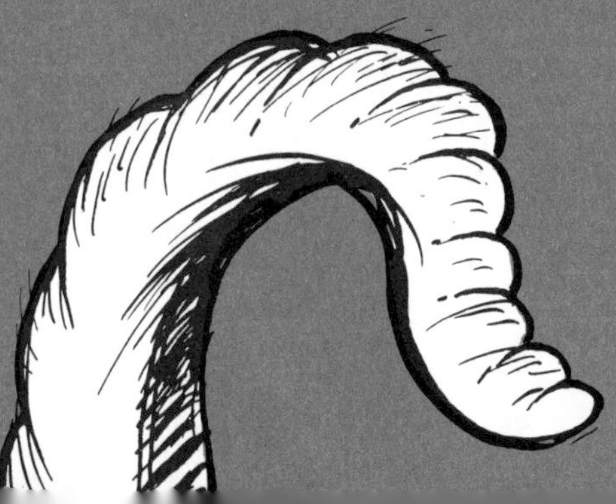

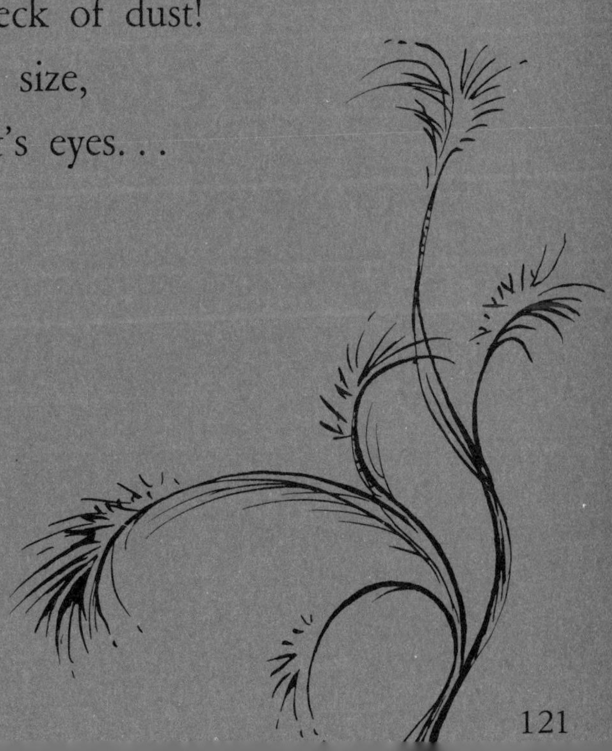

"... some poor little person who's shaking with fear
That he'll blow in the pool! He has no way to steer!
I'll just have to save him. Because, after all,
A person's a person, no matter how small."

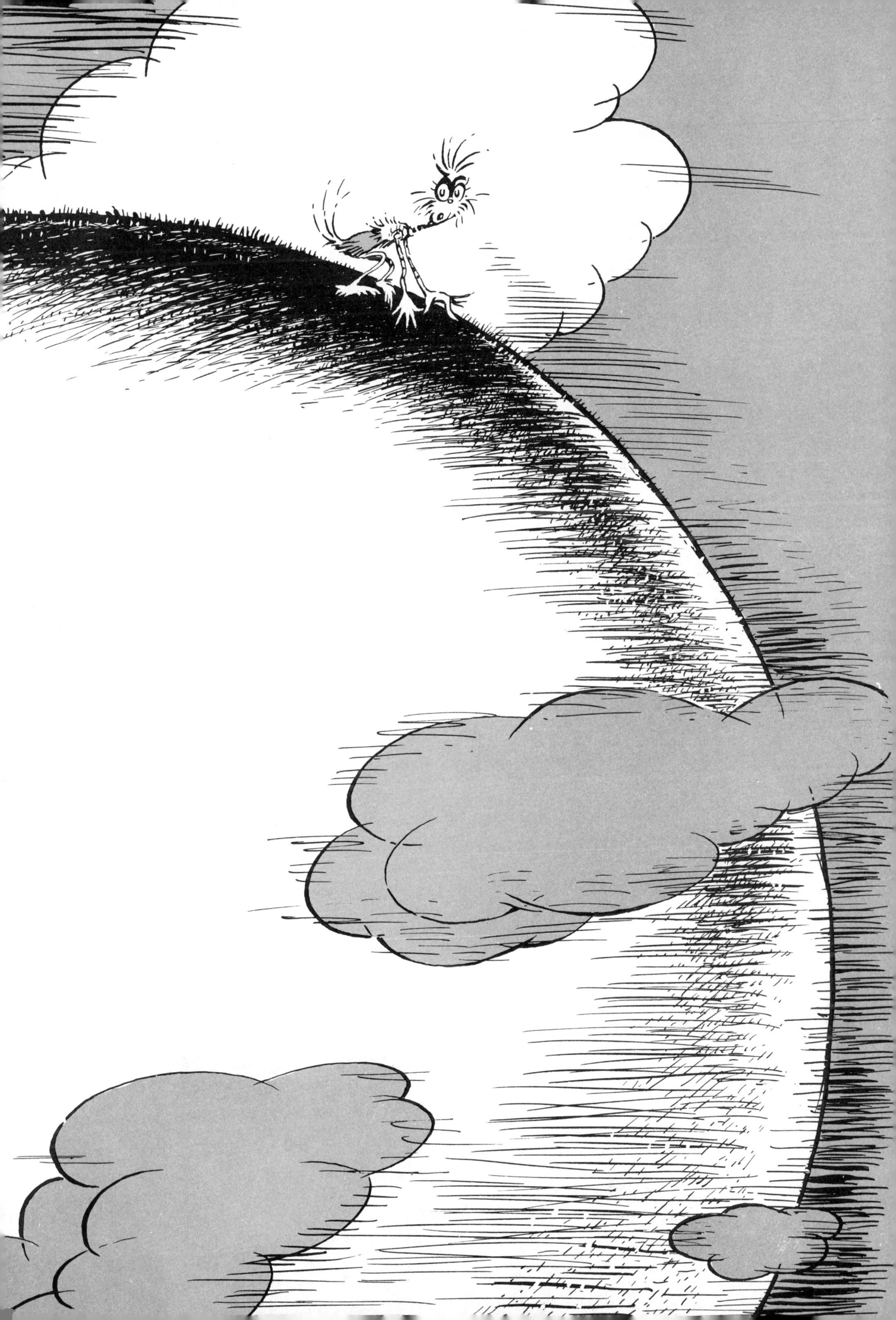

So, gently, and using the greatest of care,
The elephant stretched his great trunk through the air,
And he lifted the dust speck and carried it over
And placed it down, safe, on a very soft clover.

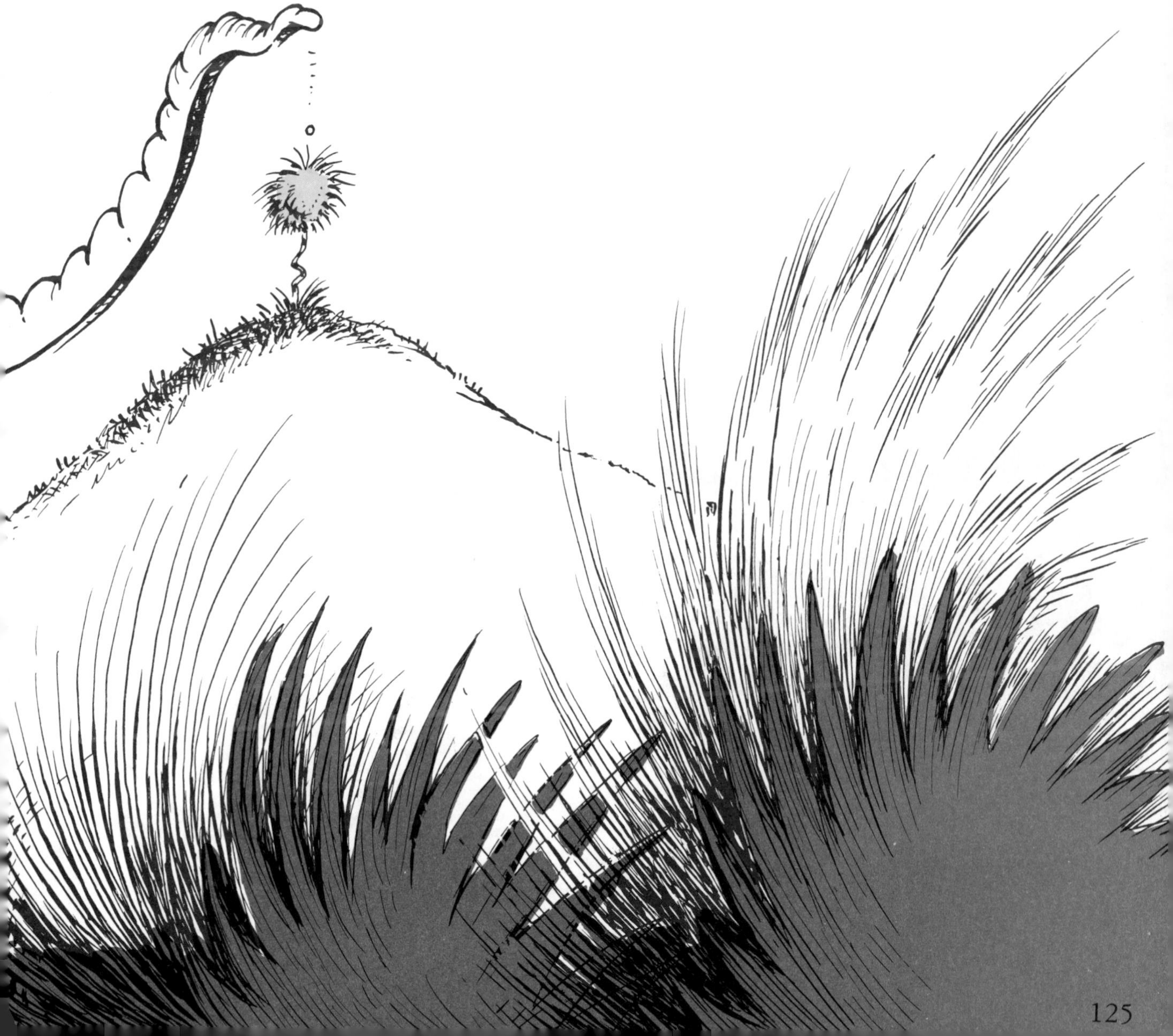

"Humpf!" humpfed a voice. 'Twas a sour kangaroo.
And the young kangaroo in her pouch said "Humpf!" too.
"Why, that speck is as small as the head of a pin.
A person on *that?*... Why, there never has been!"

"Believe me," said Horton. "I tell you sincerely,
My ears are quite keen and I heard him quite clearly.
I *know* there's a person down there. And, what's more,
Quite likely there's two. Even three. Even four.
Quite likely . . .

". . . a family, for all that we know!
A family with children just starting to grow.
So, please," Horton said, "as a favor to me,
Try not to disturb them. Just please let them be."

"I think you're a fool!" laughed the sour kangaroo
And the young kangaroo in her pouch said, "Me, too!
You're the biggest blame fool in the Jungle of Nool!"
And the kangaroos plunged in the cool of the pool.
"What terrible splashing!" the elephant frowned.
"I can't let my very small persons get drowned!
I've *got* to protect them. I'm bigger than they."
So he plucked up the clover and hustled away.

Through the high jungle tree tops, the news quickly spread:
"He talks to a dust speck! He's out of his head!
Just look at him walk with that speck on that flower!"
And Horton walked, worrying, almost an hour.
"Should I put this speck down? . . ." Horton thought with alarm.
"If I do, these small persons may come to great harm.
I *can't* put it down. And I *won't!* After all
A person's a person. No matter how small."

Then Horton stopped walking.
The speck-voice was talking!
The voice was so faint he could just barely hear it.
"Speak *up,* please," said Horton. He put his ear near it.

"My friend," came the voice, "you're a *very* fine friend.
You've helped all us folks on this dust speck no end.
You've saved all our houses, our ceilings and floors.
You've saved all our churches and grocery stores."

"You mean . . ." Horton gasped, "you have *buildings* there, *too?*"

"Oh, yes," piped the voice. "We most certainly do. . . .
"I know," called the voice, "I'm too small to be seen
But I'm Mayor of a town that is friendly and clean.
Our buildings, to you, would seem terribly small
But to us, who aren't big, they are wonderfully tall.
My town is called *Who*-ville, for I am a *Who*
And we *Whos* are all thankful and grateful to you."

And Horton called back to the Mayor of the town,
"You're safe now. Don't worry. I won't let you down."

But, just as he spoke to the Mayor of the speck,
Three big jungle monkeys climbed up Horton's neck!
The Wickersham Brothers came shouting, "What rot!
This elephant's talking to *Whos* who are *not!*
There *aren't* any *Whos!* And they *don't* have a Mayor!
And *we're* going to stop all this nonsense! *So there!*"

They snatched Horton's clover! They carried it off
To a black-bottomed eagle named Vlad Vlad-i-koff,
A mighty strong eagle, of very swift wing,
And they said, "Will you kindly get rid of this thing?"
And, before the poor elephant even could speak,
That eagle flew off with the flower in his beak.

All that late afternoon and far into the night
That black-bottomed bird flapped his wings in fast flight,
While Horton chased after, with groans, over stones
That tattered his toenails and battered his bones,
And begged, "Please don't harm all my little folks, who
Have as much right to live as us bigger folks do!"

But far, far beyond him, that eagle kept flapping
And over his shoulder called back, "Quit your yapping.
I'll fly the night through. I'm a bird. I don't mind it.
And I'll hide this, tomorrow, where *you'll* never find it!"

And at 6:56 the next morning he did it.
It sure was a terrible place that he hid it.
He let that small clover drop somewhere inside
Of a great patch of clovers a hundred miles wide!
"Find THAT!" sneered the bird. "But I think you will fail."
And he left
With a flip
Of his black-bottomed tail.

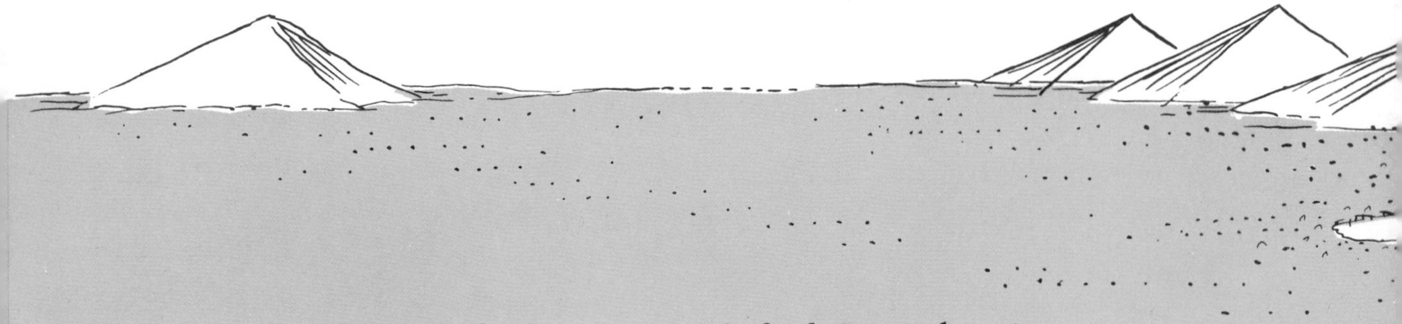

"I'll find it!" cried Horton. "I'll find it or bust!
I SHALL find my friends on my small speck of dust!"
And clover, by clover, by clover with care
He picked up and searched them, and called, "Are you there?"
But clover, by clover, by clover he found
That the one that he sought for was just not around.
And by noon poor old Horton, more dead than alive,
Had picked, searched, and piled up, nine thousand and five.

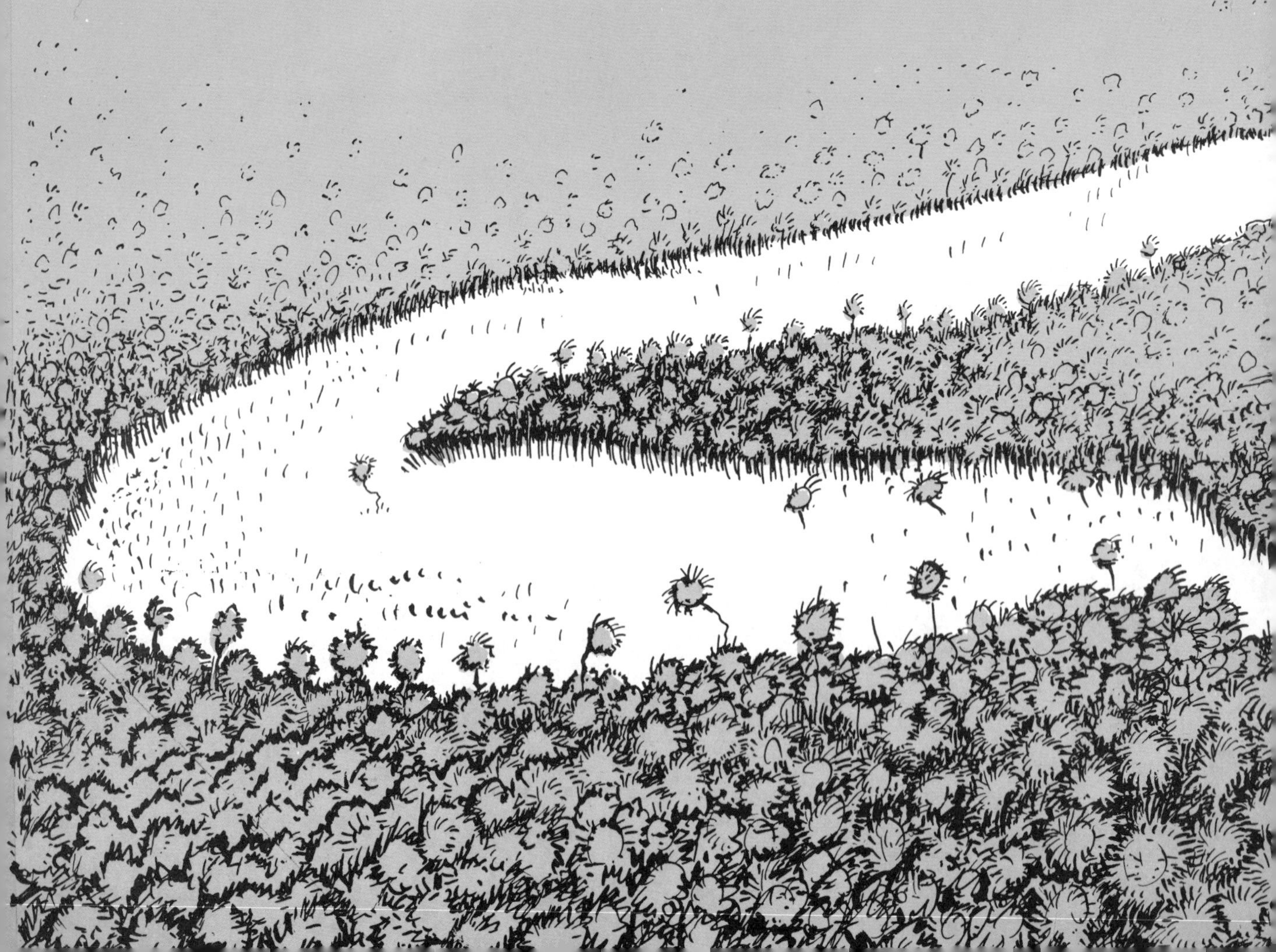

Then, on through the afternoon, hour after hour . . .
Till he found them at last! On the three millionth flower!
"My friends!" cried the elephant. "Tell me! Do tell!
Are you safe? Are you sound? Are you whole? Are you well?"

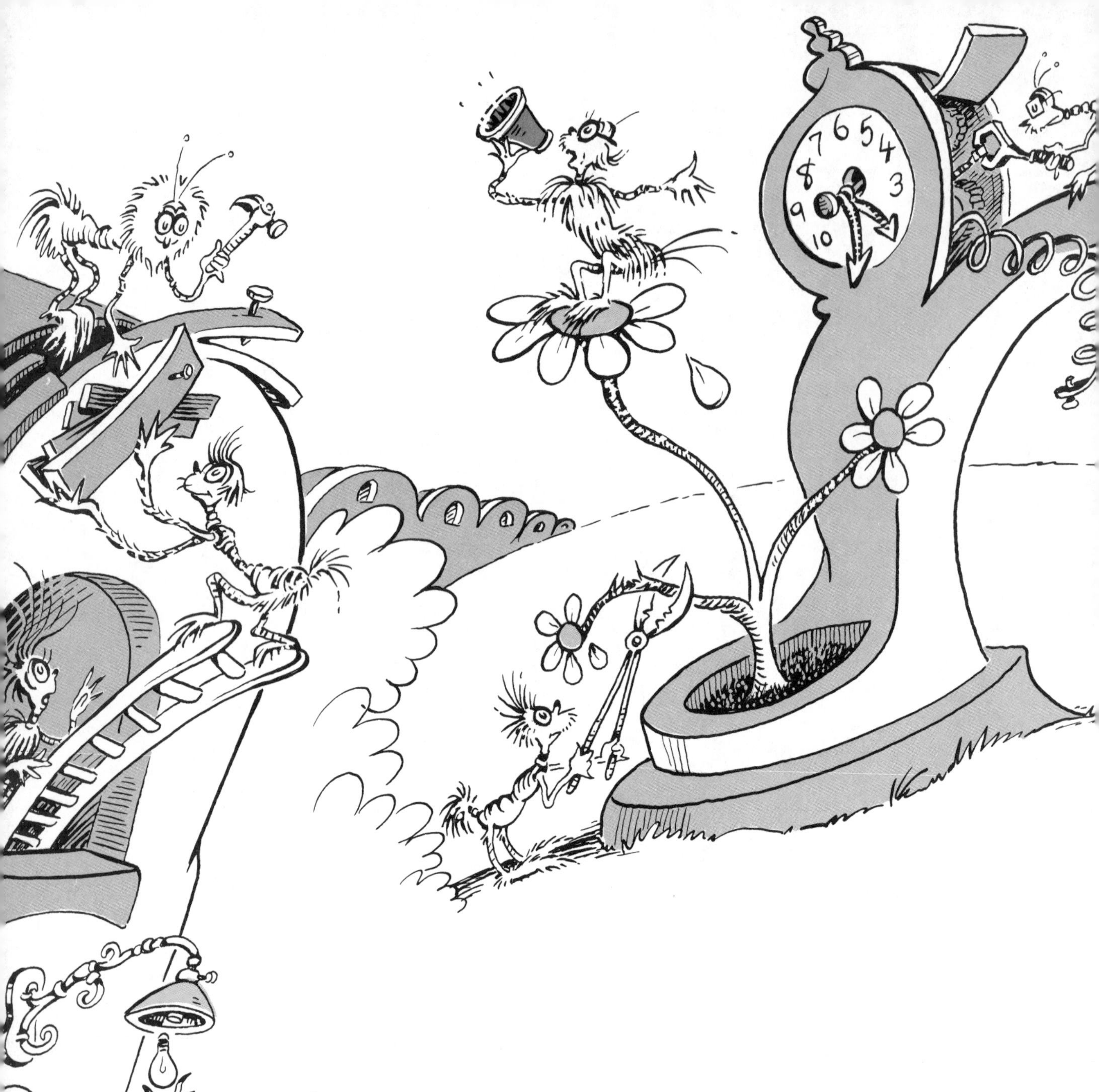

From down on the speck came the voice of the Mayor:

"We've *really* had trouble! Much more than our share.
When that black-bottomed birdie let go and we dropped,
We landed so hard that our clocks have all stopped.
Our tea-pots are broken. Our rocking-chairs smashed.
And our bicycle tires all blew up when we crashed.
So, Horton, *please!*" pleaded that voice of the Mayor's,
"Will you stick by us *Whos* while we're making repairs?"

"Of course," Horton answered. "Of course I will stick.
I'll stick by you small folks through thin and through thick!"

"Humpf!"
Humpfed a voice!
"For almost two days you've run wild and insisted
On chatting with persons who've never existed.
Such carryings-on in our peaceable jungle!
We've had quite enough of your bellowing bungle!
And I'm here to state," snapped the big kangaroo,
"That your silly nonsensical game is all through!"
And the young kangaroo in her pouch said, "Me, too!"

"With the help of the Wickersham Brothers and dozens
Of Wickersham Uncles and Wickersham Cousins
And Wickersham In-Laws, whose help I've engaged,
You're going to be roped! And you're going to be caged!
And, as for your dust speck . . . *hah! That* we shall boil
In a hot steaming kettle of Beezle-Nut oil!"

"Boil it? . . ." gasped Horton!
"Oh, that you *can't* do!
It's all full of persons!
They'll *prove* it to you!"

"Mr. Mayor! Mr. Mayor!" Horton called. "Mr. Mayor!
You've *got* to prove now that you really are there!
So call a big meeting. Get everyone out.
Make every *Who* holler! Make every *Who* shout!
Make every *Who* scream! If you don't, every *Who*
Is going to end up in a Beezle-Nut stew!"

And, down on the dust speck, the scared little Mayor
Quick called a big meeting in *Who*-ville Town Square.
And his people cried loudly. They cried out in fear:
"We are here! We are here! We are here! We are here!"

The elephant smiled: "That was clear as a bell.
You kangaroos surely heard *that* very well."
"All I heard," snapped the big kangaroo, "was the breeze,
And the faint sound of wind through the far-distant trees.
I heard no small voices. And you didn't either."
And the young kangaroo in her pouch said, "Me, neither."

"Grab him!" they shouted. "And cage the big dope!
Lasso his stomach with ten miles of rope!
Tie the knots tight so he'll *never* shake loose!
Then dunk that dumb speck in the Beezle-Nut juice!"

Horton fought back with great vigor and vim
But the Wickersham gang was too many for him.
They beat him! They mauled him! They started to haul
Him into his cage! But he managed to call
To the Mayor: "Don't give up! I believe in you all!
A person's a person, no matter how small!
And you very small persons will *not* have to die
If you make yourselves heard! *So come on, now, and TRY!"*

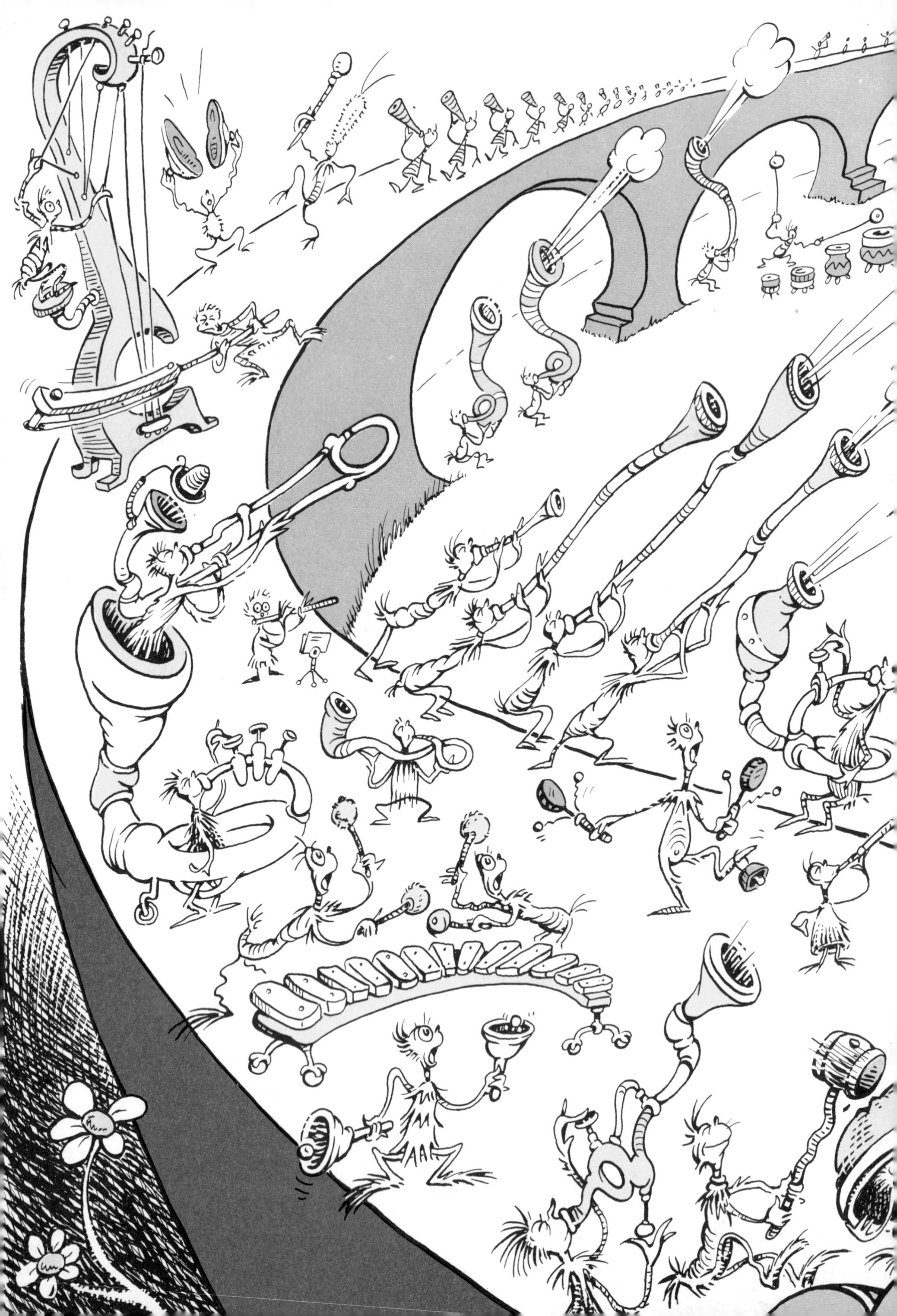

The Mayor grabbed a tom-tom. He started to smack it.
And, all over *Who*-ville, they whooped up a racket.
They rattled tin kettles! They beat on brass pans,
On garbage pail tops and old cranberry cans!
They blew on bazookas and blasted great toots
On clarinets, oom-pahs and boom-pahs and flutes!

Great gusts of loud racket rang high through the air.
They rattled and shook the whole sky! And the Mayor
Called up through the howling mad hullabaloo:
"Hey, Horton! *How's this?* Is our sound coming through?"

And Horton called back, "I can hear you just fine.
But the kangaroos' ears aren't as strong, quite, as mine.
They don't hear a thing! Are you *sure* all your boys
Are doing their best? Are they ALL making noise?
Are you sure every *Who* down in *Who*-ville is working?
Quick! Look through your town! Is there anyone shirking?"

Through the town rushed the Mayor, from the east to the west.
But *everyone* seemed to be doing his best.
Everyone seemed to be yapping or yipping!
Everyone seemed to be beeping or bipping!
But it *wasn't enough,* all this ruckus and roar!
He HAD to find someone to help him make more.
He raced through each building! He searched floor-to-floor!

And, just as he felt he was getting nowhere,
And almost about to give up in despair,
He suddenly burst through a door and that Mayor
Discovered one shirker! Quite hidden away
In the Fairfax Apartments (Apartment 12-J)
A very small, *very* small shirker named Jo-Jo
Was standing, just standing, and bouncing a Yo-Yo!
Not making a sound! Not a yipp! Not a chirp!
And the Mayor rushed inside and he grabbed the young twerp!

APT.
12-J

And he climbed with the lad up the Eiffelberg Tower.

"This," cried the Mayor, "is your town's darkest hour!
The time for all *Whos* who have blood that is red
To come to the aid of their country!" he said.
"We've GOT to make noises in greater amounts!
So, open your mouth, lad! For every voice counts!"

Thus he spoke as he climbed. When they got to the top,
The lad cleared his throat and he shouted out, "YOPP!"

And that Yopp...
That one small, extra Yopp put it over!
Finally, at last! From that speck on that clover
Their voices were heard! They rang out clear and clean.
And the elephant smiled. "Do you see what I mean?...
They've proved they ARE persons, no matter how small.
And their whole world was saved by the Smallest of All!"

"How true! Yes, how true," said the big kangaroo.
"And, from now on, you know what I'm planning to do?...
From now on, I'm going to protect them with you!"
And the young kangaroo in her pouch said,...

"... ME, TOO!
From sun in the summer. From rain when it's fall-ish,
I'm going to protect them. No matter how small-ish!"

The SNEETCHES AND OTHER STORIES

The
SNEETCHES

Now, the Star-Belly Sneetches
Had bellies with stars.
The Plain-Belly Sneetches
Had none upon thars.

Those stars weren't so big. They were really so small
You might think such a thing wouldn't matter at all.

But, because they had stars, all the Star-Belly Sneetches
Would brag, "We're the best kind of Sneetch on the beaches."
With their snoots in the air, they would sniff and they'd snort
"We'll have nothing to do with the Plain-Belly sort!"
And whenever they met some, when they were out walking,
They'd hike right on past them without even talking.

When the Star-Belly children went out to play ball,
Could a Plain Belly get in the game...? Not at all.
You only could play if your bellies had stars
And the Plain-Belly children had none upon thars.

When the Star-Belly Sneetches had frankfurter roasts
Or picnics or parties or marshmallow toasts,
They never invited the Plain-Belly Sneetches.
They left them out cold, in the dark of the beaches.
They kept them away. Never let them come near.
And that's how they treated them year after year.

Then ONE day, it seems... while the Plain-Belly Sneetches
Were moping and doping alone on the beaches,
Just sitting there wishing their bellies had stars...
A stranger zipped up in the strangest of cars!

"My friends," he announced in a voice clear and keen,
"My name is Sylvester McMonkey McBean.
And I've heard of your troubles. I've heard you're unhappy.
But I can fix that. I'm the Fix-it-Up Chappie.
I've come here to help you. I have what you need.
And my prices are low. And I work at great speed.
And my work is one hundred per cent guaranteed!"

Then, quickly, Sylvester McMonkey McBean
Put together a very peculiar machine.
And he said, "You want stars like a Star-Belly Sneetch...?
My friends, you can have them for three dollars each!"

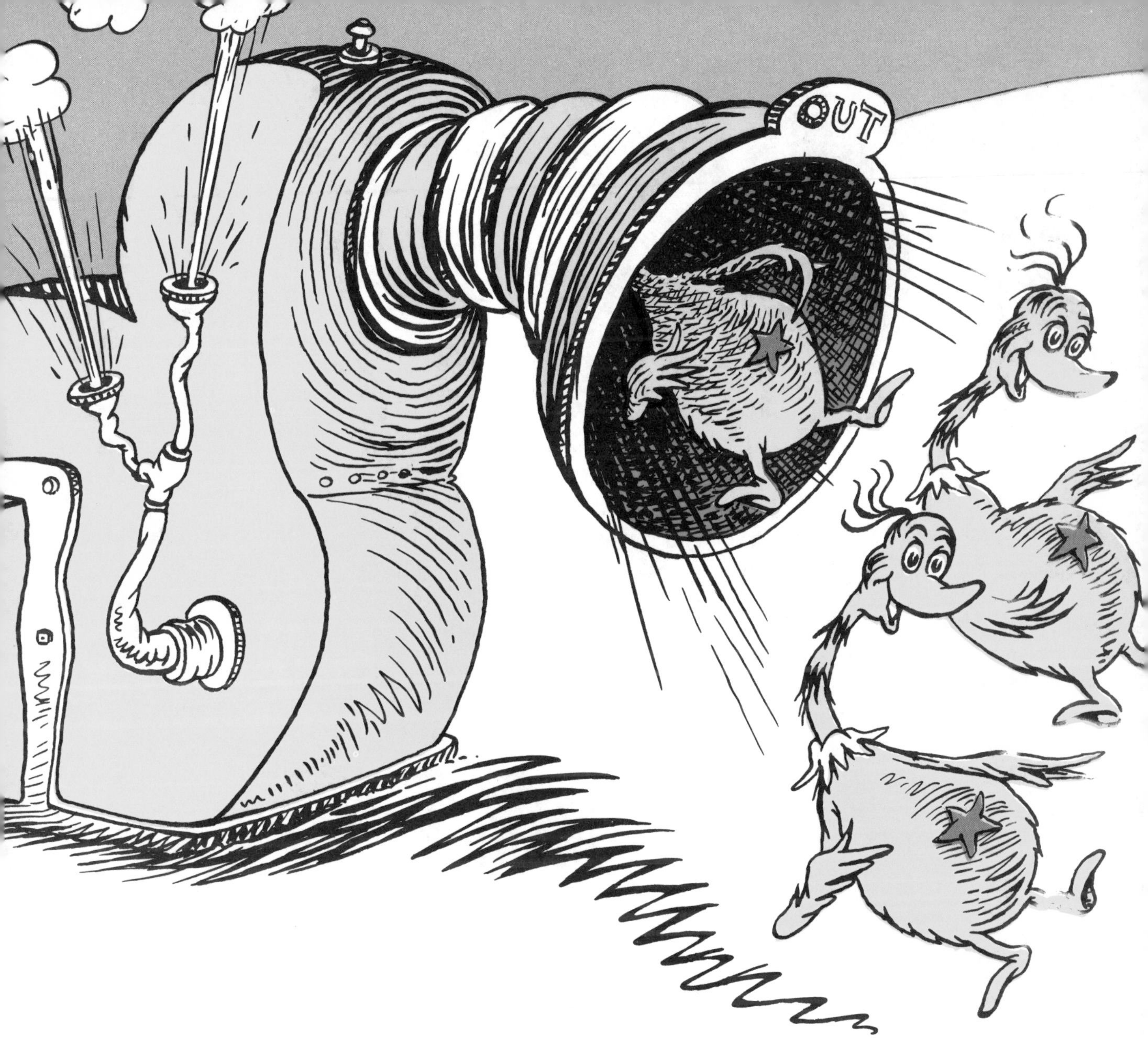

"Just pay me your money and hop right aboard!"
So they clambered inside. Then the big machine roared
And it klonked. And it bonked. And it jerked. And it berked
And it bopped them about. But the thing really worked!
When the Plain-Belly Sneetches popped out, they had stars!
They actually did. They had stars upon thars!

Then they yelled at the ones who had stars at the start,
"We're exactly like you! You can't tell us apart.
We're all just the same, now, you snooty old smarties!
And now we can go to your frankfurter parties."

"Good grief!" groaned the ones who had stars at the first.
"We're *still* the best Sneetches and they are the worst.
But, now, how in the world will we know," they all frowned,
"If which kind is what, or the other way round?"

Then up came McBean with a very sly wink
And he said, "Things are not quite as bad as you think.
So you don't know who's who. That is perfectly true.
But come with me, friends. Do you know what I'll do?
I'll make you, again, the best Sneetches on beaches
And all it will cost you is ten dollars eaches."

IN

"Belly stars are no longer in style," said McBean.
"What you need is a trip through my Star-*Off* Machine.
This wondrous contraption will take *off* your stars
So you won't look like Sneetches who have them on thars."
And that handy machine
Working very precisely
Removed all the stars from their tummies quite nicely.

Then, with snoots in the air, they paraded about
And they opened their beaks and they let out a shout,
"We know who is who! Now there isn't a doubt.
The best kind of Sneetches are Sneetches without!"

Then, of course, those with stars all got frightfully mad.
To be wearing a star now was frightfully bad.
Then, of course, old Sylvester McMonkey McBean
Invited *them* into his Star-Off Machine.

Then, of course from THEN on, as you probably guess,
Things really got into a horrible mess.

OUT
IN
IN

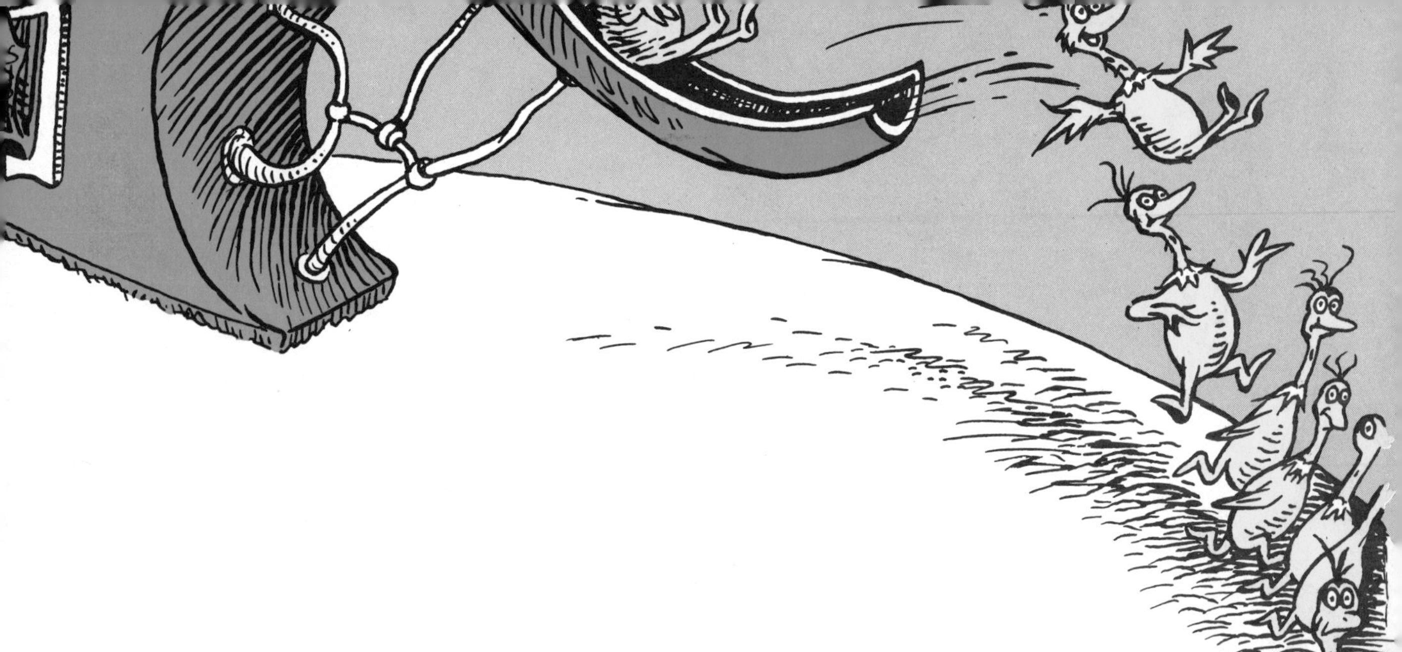

All the rest of that day, on those wild screaming beaches,
The Fix-it-Up Chappie kept fixing up Sneetches.
Off again! On again!
In again! Out again!
Through the machines they raced round and about again,
Changing their stars every minute or two.
They kept paying money. They kept running through
Until neither the Plain nor the Star-Bellies knew
Whether this one was that one . . . or that one was this one
Or which one was what one . . . or what one was who.

Then, when every last cent
Of their money was spent,
The Fix-it-Up Chappie packed up
And he went.

And he laughed as he drove
In his car up the beach,
"They never will learn.
No. You can't teach a Sneetch!"

But McBean was quite wrong. I'm quite happy to say
That the Sneetches got really quite smart on that day,
The day they decided that Sneetches are Sneetches
And no kind of Sneetch is the best on the beaches.
That day, all the Sneetches forgot about stars
And whether they had one, or not, upon thars.

THE ZAX

One day, making tracks
In the prairie of Prax,
Came a North-Going Zax
And a South-Going Zax.

And it happened that both of them came to a place
Where they bumped. There they stood.
Foot to foot. Face to face.

"Look here, now!" the North-Going Zax said. "I say!
You are blocking my path. You are right in my way.
I'm a North-Going Zax and I always go north.
Get out of my way, now, and let me go forth!"

"Who's in whose way?" snapped the South-Going Zax.
"I always go south, making south-going tracks.
So you're in MY way! And I ask you to move
And let me go south in my south-going groove."

Then the North-Going Zax puffed his chest up with pride.
"I never," he said, "take a step to one side.
And I'll prove to you that I won't change my ways
If I have to keep standing here fifty-nine days!"

"And I'll prove to YOU," yelled the South-Going Zax,
"That I can stand here in the prairie of Prax
For fifty-nine *years!* For I live by a rule
That I learned as a boy back in South-Going School.
Never budge! That's my rule. *Never budge in the least!*
Not an inch to the west! Not an inch to the east!
I'll stay here, not budging! I can and I will
If it makes you and me and the whole world stand still!"

Well . . .
Of course the world *didn't* stand still. The world grew.
In a couple of years, the new highway came through
And they built it right over those two stubborn Zax
And left them there, standing un-budged in their tracks.

Too Many Daves

Did I ever tell you that Mrs. McCave
Had twenty-three sons and she named them all Dave?

Well, she did. And that wasn't a smart thing to do.
You see, when she wants one and calls out, "Yoo-Hoo!
Come into the house, Dave!" she doesn't get *one.*
All twenty-three Daves of hers come on the run!

This makes things quite difficult at the McCaves'
As you can imagine, with so many Daves.
And often she wishes that, when they were born,
She had named one of them Bodkin Van Horn
And one of them Hoos-Foos. And one of them Snimm.
And one of them Hot-Shot. And one Sunny Jim.
And one of them Shadrack. And one of them Blinkey.
And one of them Stuffy. And one of them Stinkey.
Another one Putt-Putt. Another one Moon Face.
Another one Marvin O'Gravel Balloon Face.
And one of them Ziggy. And one Soggy Muff.
One Buffalo Bill. And one Biffalo Buff.
And one of them Sneepy. And one Weepy Weed.
And one Paris Garters. And one Harris Tweed.
And one of them Sir Michael Carmichael Zutt
And one of them Oliver Boliver Butt
And one of them Zanzibar Buck-Buck McFate...
But she didn't do it. And now it's too late.

What was I Scared of?

Well...
I was walking in the night
And I saw nothing scary.
For I have never been afraid
Of anything. Not very.

Then I was deep within the woods
When, suddenly, I spied them.
I saw a pair of pale green pants
With nobody inside them!

I wasn't scared. But, yet, I stopped.
What *could* those pants be there for?
What *could* a pair of pants at night
Be standing in the air for?

And then they moved! Those empty pants!
They kind of started jumping.
And then my heart, I must admit,
It kind of started thumping.

So I got out. I got out fast
As fast as I could go, sir.
I wasn't scared. But pants like that
I did not care for. No, sir.

After that, a week went by.
Then one dark night in Grin-itch
(I had to do an errand there
And fetch some Grin-itch spinach)...
Well, I had fetched the spinach.
I was starting back through town
When those pants raced round a corner
And they almost knocked me down!

I lost my Grin-itch spinach
But I didn't even care.
I ran for home! Believe me,
I had really had a scare!

Now, bicycles were never made
For pale green pants to ride 'em,
Especially spooky pale green pants
With nobody inside 'em!

And the NEXT night, I was fishing
For Doubt-trout on Roover River
When those pants came rowing toward me!
Well, I started in to shiver.

And by now I was SO frightened
That, I'll tell you, but I hate to...
I screamed and rowed away and lost
My hook and line and bait, too!

I ran and found a Brickel bush.
I hid myself away.
I got brickels in my britches
But I stayed there anyway.

I stayed all night. The next night. too.
I'd be there still, no doubt,
But I had to do an errand
So, the *next* night, I went out.

I had to do an errand,
Had to pick a peck of Snide
In a dark and gloomy Snide-field
That was almost nine miles wide.

I said, "I do not fear those pants
With nobody inside them."
I said, and said, and said those words.
I said them. But I lied them.

Then I reached inside a Snide bush
And the next thing that I knew,
I felt my hand touch someone!
And I'll bet that you know who.

And there I was! Caught in the Snide!
And in that dreadful place
Those spooky, empty pants and I
Were standing face to face!

I yelled for help. I screamed. I shrieked.
I howled. I yowled. I cried,
"Oh, save me from these pale green pants
With nobody inside!"

But then a strange thing happened.
Why, those pants began to cry!
Those pants began to tremble.
They were just as scared as I!

I never heard such whimpering
And I began to see
That I was just as strange to them
As they were strange to me!

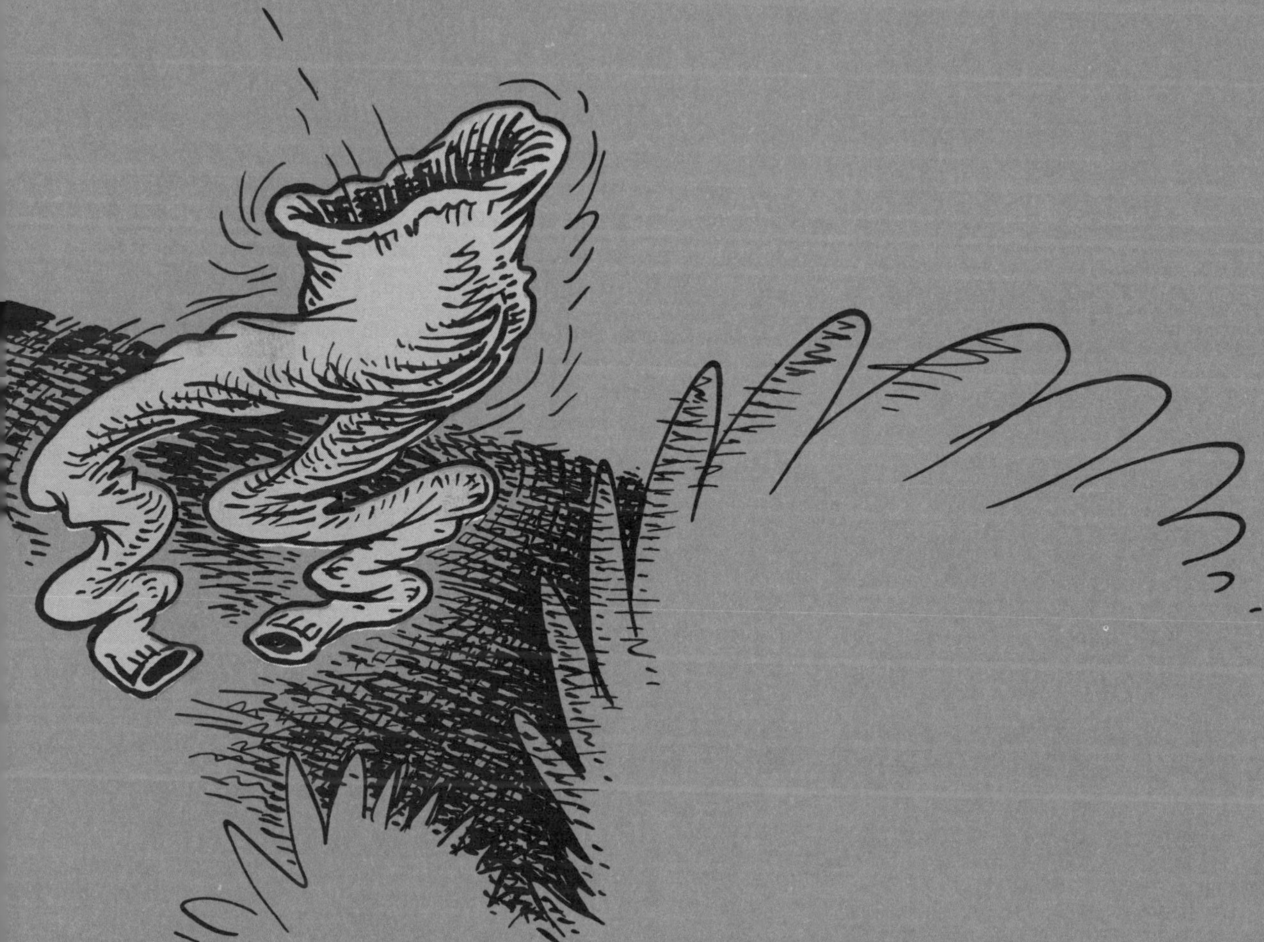

I put my arm around their waist
And sat right down beside them.
I calmed them down.
Poor empty pants
With nobody inside them.

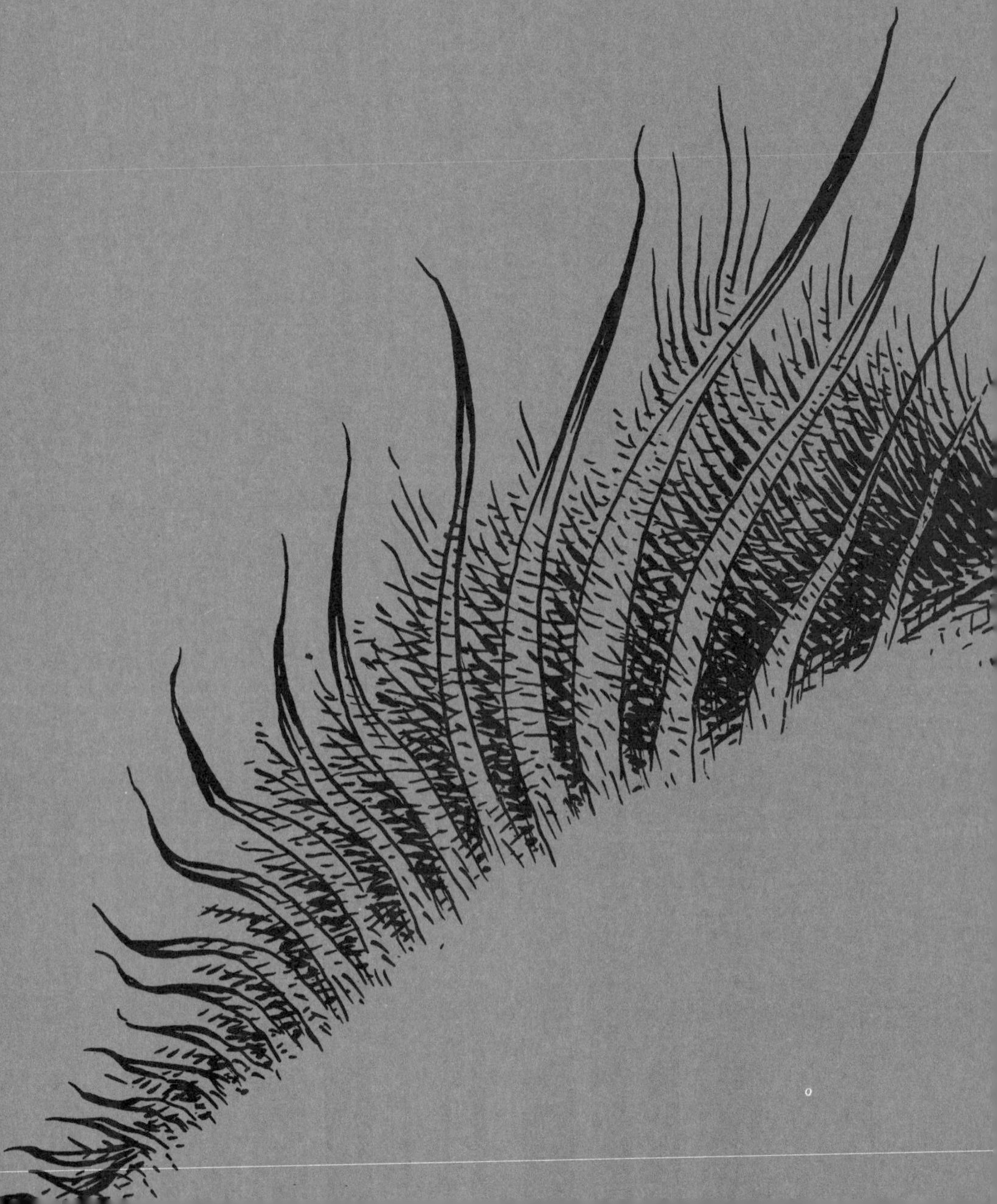

And, now, we meet quite often,
Those empty pants and I,
And we never shake or tremble.
We both smile
And we say
"Hi!"

Hi!

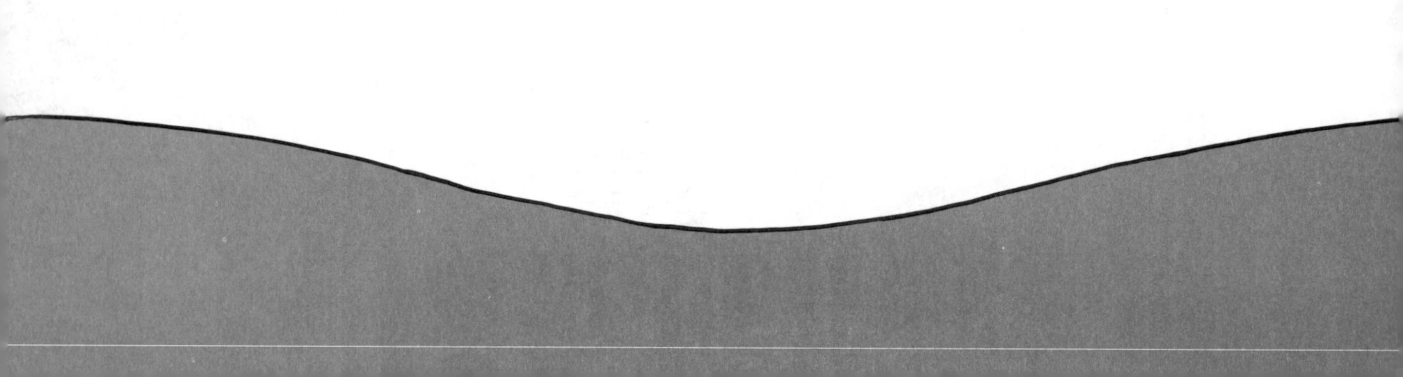

Dr. Seuss's SLEEP Book

The news
Just came in
From the County of Keck
That a very small bug
By the name of Van Vleck
Is yawning so wide
You can look down his neck.

This may not seem
Very important, I know.
But it *is.* So I'm bothering
Telling you so.

A yawn is quite catching, you see. Like a cough.
It just takes one yawn to start other yawns off.
NOW the news has come in that some friends of Van Vleck's
Are yawning so wide you can look down *their* necks.

At this moment, right now,
Under seven more noses,
Great yawns are in blossom.
They're blooming like roses.

The yawn of that one little bug is still spreading!
According to latest reports, it is heading
Across the wide fields, through the sleepy night air,
Across the whole country toward every-which-where.
And people are gradually starting to say,
"I feel rather drowsy. I've had quite a day."

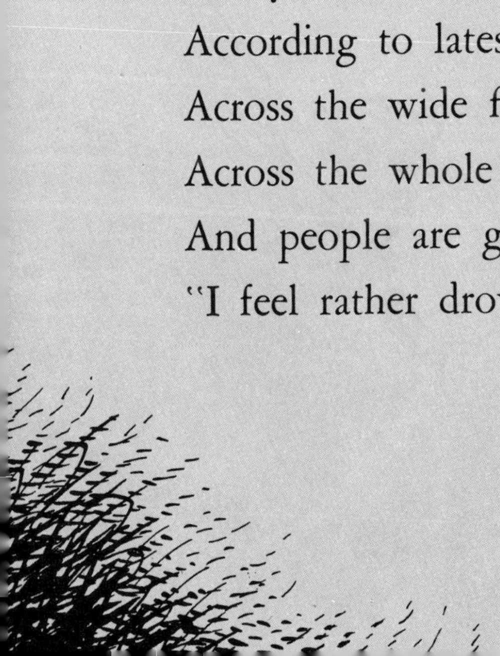

Creatures are starting to think about rest.
Two Biffer-Baum Birds are now building their nest.
They do it each night. And quite often I wonder
How they do this big job without making a blunder.
But that is *their* problem.
Not yours. And not mine.
The point is: They're going to bed.
And that's fine.

Sleep thoughts
Are spreading
Throughout the whole land.
The time for night-brushing of teeth is at hand.
Up at Herk-Heimer Falls, where the great river rushes
And crashes down crags in great gargling gushes,
The Herk-Heimer Sisters are using their brushes.
Those falls are just grand for tooth-brushing beneath
If you happen to be up that way with your teeth.

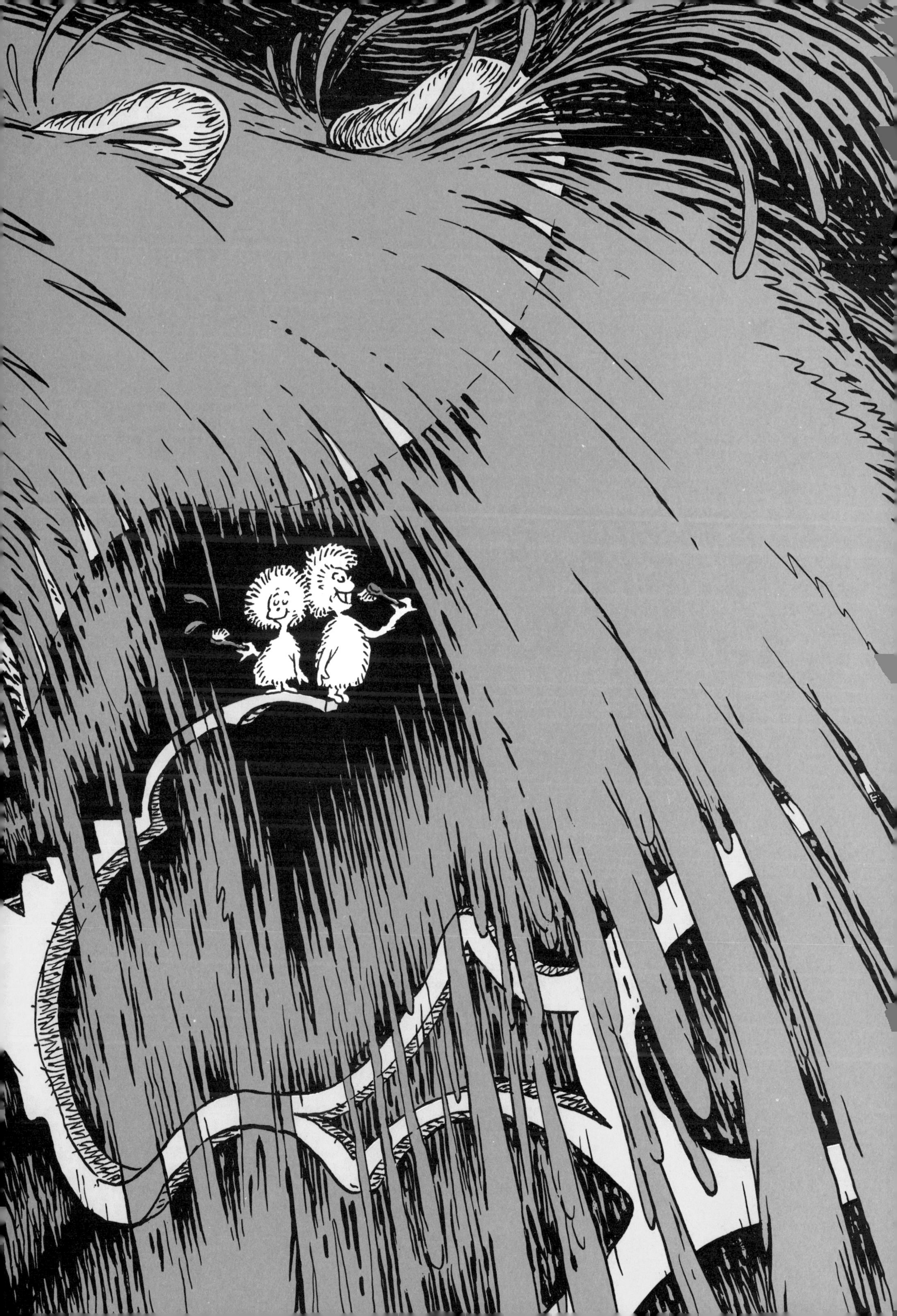

The news just came in from the Castle of Krupp
That the lights are all out and the drawbridge is up.
And the old drawbridge draw-er just said with a yawn,
"My drawbridge is drawn and it's going to stay drawn
'Til the milkman delivers the milk, about dawn.
I'm going to bed now. So nobody better
Come round with a special delivery letter."

The number
Of sleepers
Is steadily growing.
Bed is where
More and more people are going.
In Culpepper Springs, in the Stilt-Walkers' Hall,
The stilt-walkers' stilts are all stacked on the wall.
The stilt-walker walkers have called it a day.
They're all tuckered out and they're snoozing away.
This is very big news. It's important to know.
And that's why I'm bothering telling you so.

Way out in the west, in the town of Mercedd,
The Hinkle-Horn Honking Club just went to bed.
Every horn has been quietly hung on a hook,
For the night, in its own private Hinkle-Horn Nook.

All this long, happy day, they've been honking about
And the Hinkle-Horn Honkers have honked themselves out.
But they'll wake up quite fresh in the morning. And then...
They'll start right in Hinkle-Horn honking again.

Everywhere, creatures
Are falling asleep.
The Collapsible Frink
Just collapsed in a heap.
And, by adding the Frink
To the others before,
I am able to give you
The Who's-Asleep-Score:
Right now, forty thousand
Four hundred and four
Creatures are happily,
Deeply in slumber.
I think you'll agree
That's a whopping fine number.

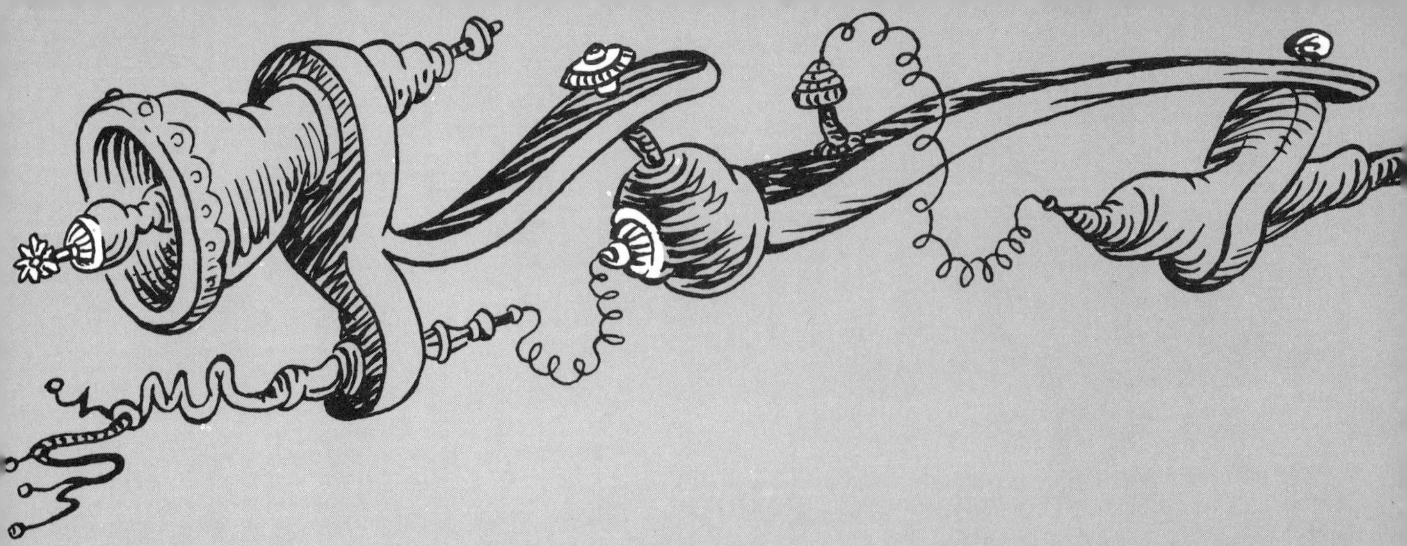

Counting up sleepers . . ?
Just how do we do it . . ?
Really quite simple. There's nothing much to it.
We find out how many, we learn the amount
By an Audio-Telly-o-Tally-o Count.
On a mountain, halfway between Reno and Rome,
We have a machine in a plexiglass dome
Which listens and looks into everyone's home.
And whenever it sees a new sleeper go flop,
It jiggles and lets a new Biggel-Ball drop.
Our chap counts these balls as they plup in a cup.
And that's how we know who is down and who's up.

40, 404

Do you talk in your sleep . . ?
It's a wonderful sport
And I have some news of this sport to report.
The World-Champion Sleep-Talkers, Jo and Mo Redd-Zoff,
Have just gone to sleep and they're talking their heads off.
For fifty-five years, now, each chattering brother
Has babbled and gabbled all night to the other.

They've talked about laws and they've talked about gauze.
They've talked about paws and they've talked about flaws.
They've talked quite a lot about old Santa Claus.
And the reason I'm telling you this is because
You should take up this sport. It's just fine for the jaws.

Do you walk in your sleep . . ?
I just had a report
Of some interesting news of this popular sport.
Near Finnigan Fen, there's a sleepwalking group
Which not only walks, but it walks a-la-hoop!
Every night they go miles. Why, they walk to such length
They have to keep eating to keep up their strength.

So, every so often, one puts down his hoop,
Stops hooping and does some quick snooping for soup.
That's why they are known as the Hoop-Soup-Snoop Group.

Sleepwalking, too, are the Curious Crandalls
Who sleepwalk on hills with assorted-sized candles.
The Crandalls walk nightly in slumbering peace
In spite of slight burns from the hot dripping grease.
The Crandalls wear candles because they walk far
And, if they wake up,
Want to see where they are.

Now the news has arrived
From the Valley of Vail
That a Chippendale Mupp has just bitten his tail,
Which he does every night before shutting his eyes.
Such nipping sounds silly. But, really, it's wise.

He has no alarm clock. So this is the way
He makes sure that he'll wake at the right time of day.
His tail is so long, he won't feel any pain
'Til the nip makes the trip and gets up to his brain.
In exactly eight hours, the Chippendale Mupp
Will, at last, feel the bite and yell "Ouch!" and wake up.

A Mr. and Mrs. J. Carmichael Krox
Have just gone to bed near the town of Fort Knox.
And they, by the way, have the finest of clocks.

I'm not at all sure that I quite quite understand
Just how the thing works, with that one extra hand.
But I *do* know this clock does one very slick trick.
It doesn't tick tock. How it goes, is tock tick.
So, with ticks in its tocker, and tocks in its ticker
It saves lots of time and the sleepers sleep quicker.

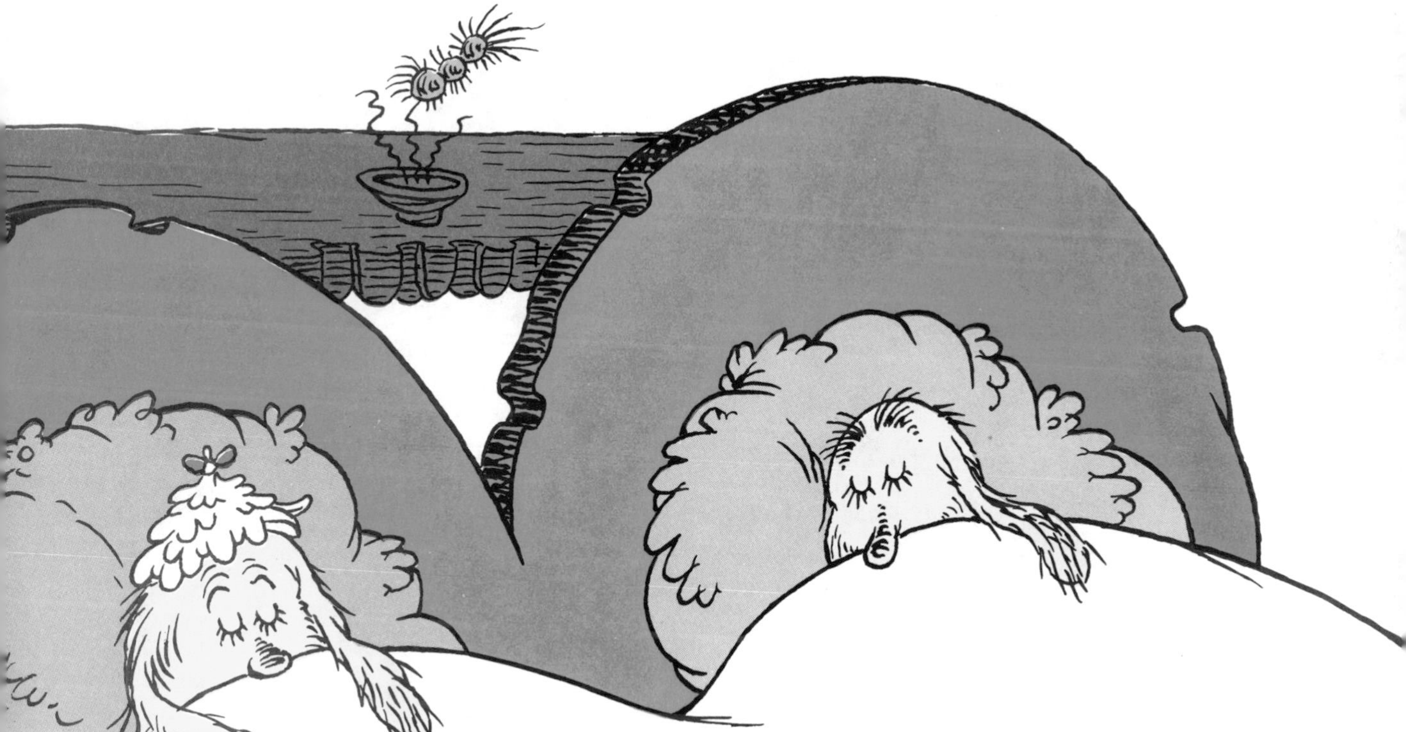

What a fine night for sleeping! From all that I hear,
It's the best night for sleeping in many a year.
They're even asleep in the Zwieback Motel!
And people don't usually sleep there too well.

The beds are like rocks and, as everyone knows,
The sheets are too short. They won't cover your toes.
SO, if people are actually sleeping in THERE...
It's a great night for sleeping! It must be the air.

It's a great night for snores! I just had a report
Of some boys who are tops in this musical sport.
The snortiest snorers in all our fair land
Are Snorter McPhail and his Snore-a-Snort Band.
This band can snore *Dixie* and old *Swanee River*
So loud it would make forty elephants shiver.

The loudest of all of the boys is McPhail.
HE snores with his head in a three-gallon pail.
So they snore in a cave twenty miles out of town.
If they snored closer in, they would snore the town down.

Do you know who's asleep
Out in Foona-Lagoona . . ?
Two very nice
Foona-Lagoona Baboona.

We've added them into our Who's-Asleep Count
Which has grown to a really amazing amount.
Exactly eight million, eight hundred and eight
Creatures are sleeping now! Isn't that great!

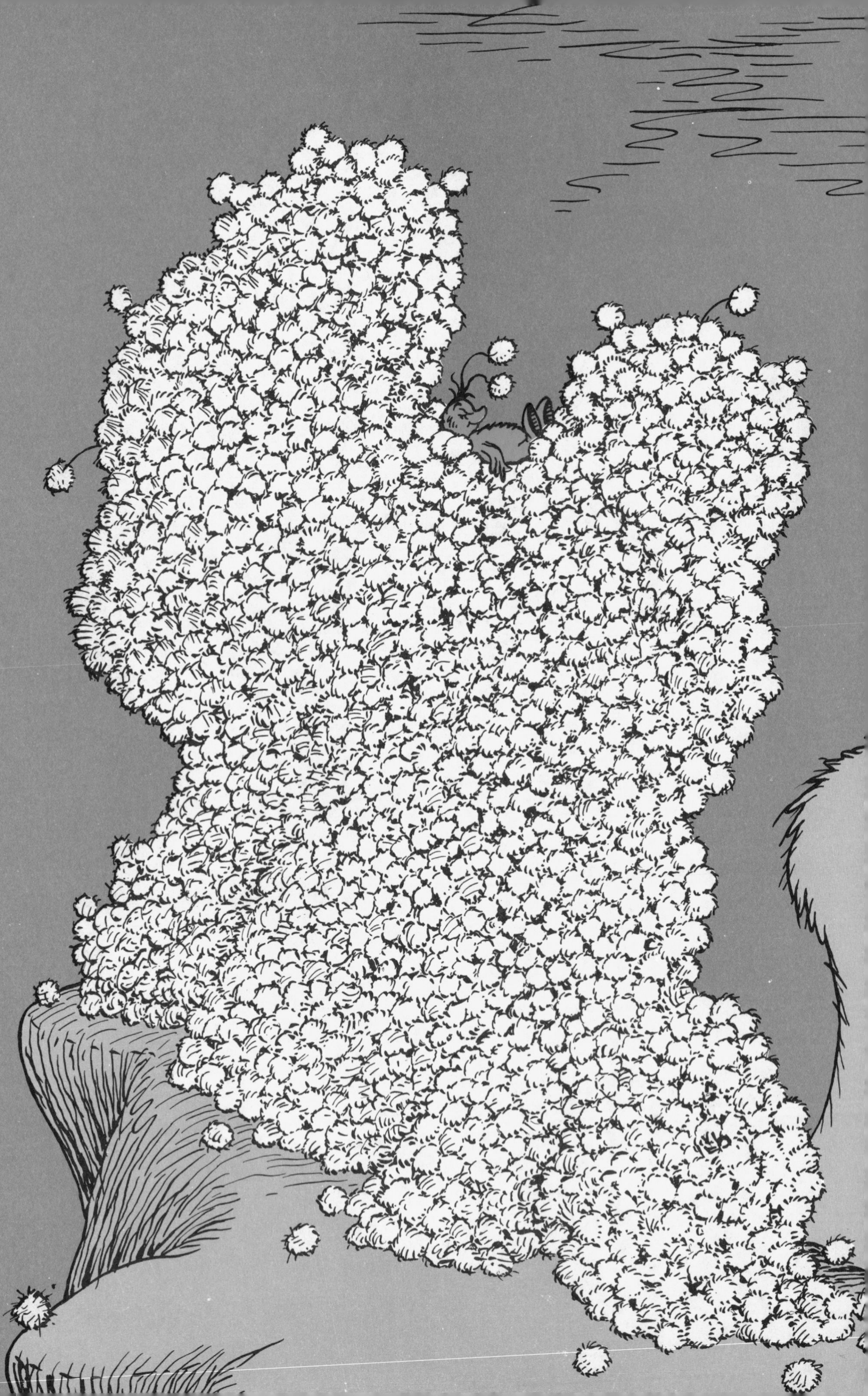

A Jedd is in bed,
And the bed of a Jedd
Is the softest
Of beds in the world,
It is said.
He makes it from pom poms
He grows on his head.
And he's sleeping right now
On the softest of fluff,
Completely exhausted
From growing the stuff.

The news has come in from the District of Dofft
That two Offt are asleep and they're sleeping aloft.
And how are they able to sleep off the ground..?
I'll tell you. I weighed one last week and I found
That an Offt is SO light he weighs minus one pound!

THIS ONE, TOO, PLEASE

A moose is asleep.
He is dreaming of moose drinks.
A goose is asleep.
He is dreaming of goose drinks.
That's well and good when a moose dreams of moose juice.
And nothing goes wrong when a goose dreams of goose juice.

But it isn't too good when a moose and a goose
Start dreaming they're drinking the other one's juice.
Moose juice, not goose juice, is juice for a moose
And goose juice, not moose juice, is juice for a goose.
So, when goose gets a mouthful of juices of moose's
And moose gets a mouthful of juices of goose's,
They always fall out of their beds screaming screams.
SO . . .
I'm warning you, now! Never drink in your dreams.

Speaking of dreaming,
I think you should note
That the Bumble-Tub Club Is now dreaming afloat.
Every night they go dreaming down Bumble-Tub Creek
Except for one night, every third or fourth week,
When they stop for repairs. 'Cause their bumble-tubs leak.
But tonight they're afloat, full of dreams, full of bliss,
And that's why I'm bothering telling you this.

At the fork of a road
In the Vale of Va-Vode
Five foot-weary salesmen have laid down their load.
All day they've raced round in the heat, at top speeds,
Unsuccessfully trying to sell Zizzer-Zoof Seeds
Which nobody wants because nobody needs.

Tomorrow will come. They'll go back to their chore.
They'll start on the road, Zizzer-Zoofing once more
But tonight they've forgotten their feet are so sore.
And that's what the wonderful night time is for.

Everywhere,
Creatures
Have shut off their voices.
They've all gone to bed
In the beds of their choices.

They're sleeping in bushes. They're sleeping in crannies.
Some on their stomachs, and some on their fannies.
They're peacefully sleeping in comfortable holes.
Some, even, on soft-tufted barber shop poles.
The number of sleepers is now past the millions!
The number of sleepers is now in the billions!

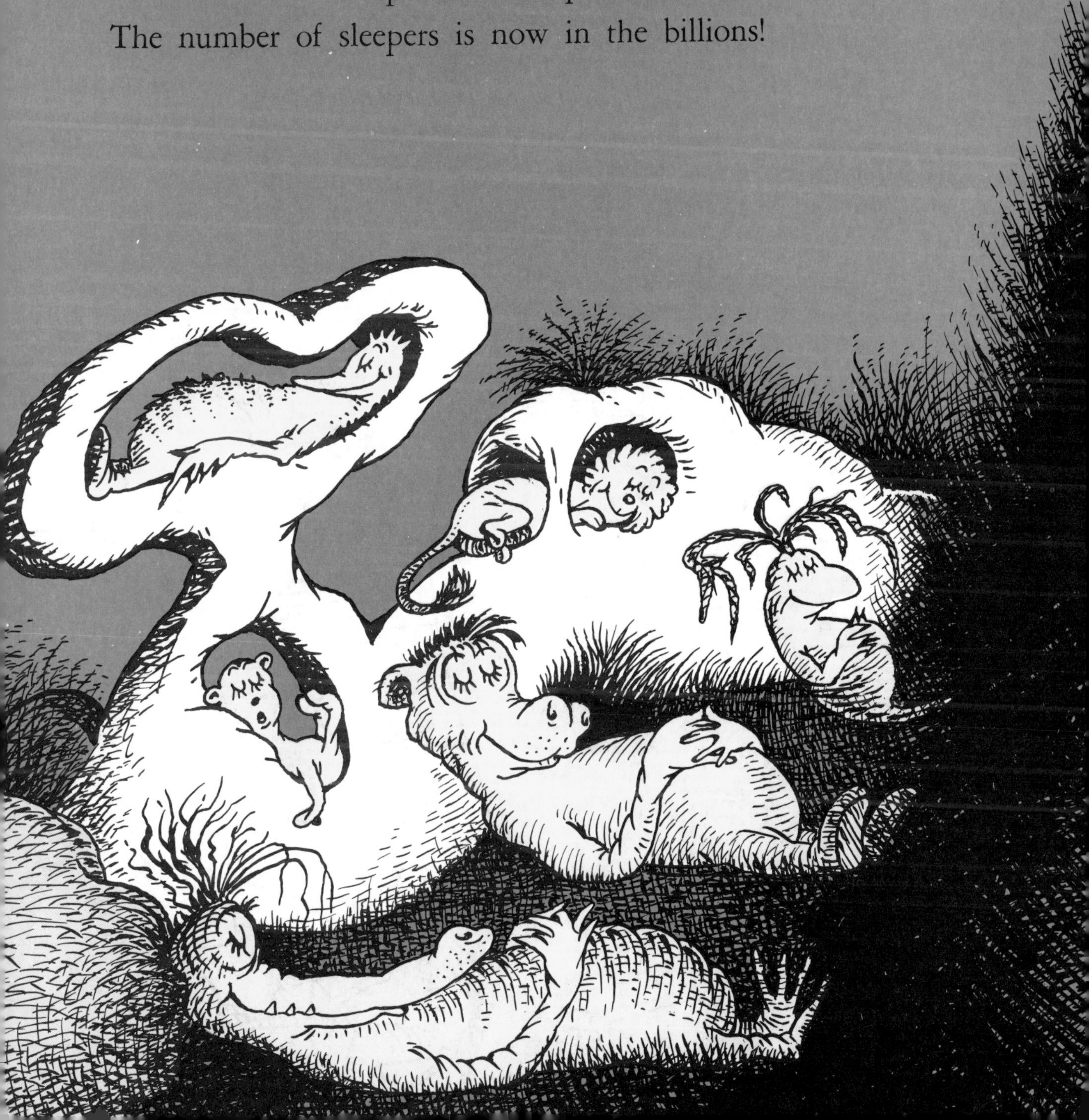

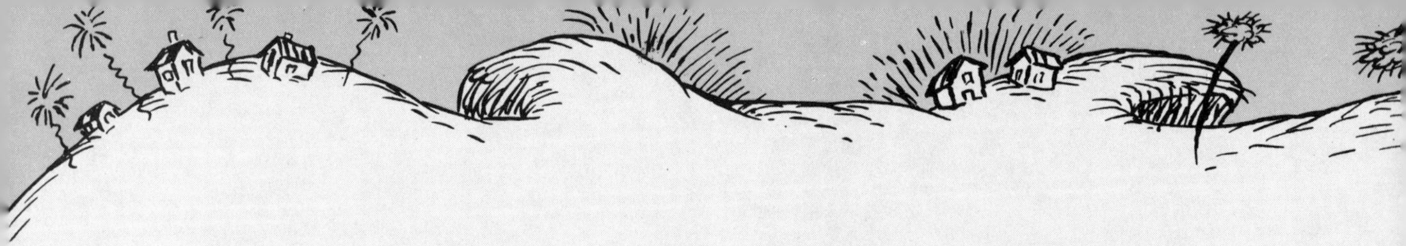

They're sleeping on steps! And on strings! And on floors!
In mailboxes, ships, and the keyholes of doors!
Every worm on a fishhook is safe for the night.
Every fish in the sea is too sleepy to bite.
Every whale in the ocean has turned off his spout.
Every light between here and Far Foodle is out.
And now, adding things up, we are way beyond billions!
Our Who's-Asleep-Score is now up in the Zillions!

Ninety-nine zillion,
Nine trillion and two
Creatures are sleeping!
So . . .
How about you?

When you put out *your* light,
Then the number will be
Ninety-nine zillion
Nine trillion and three.

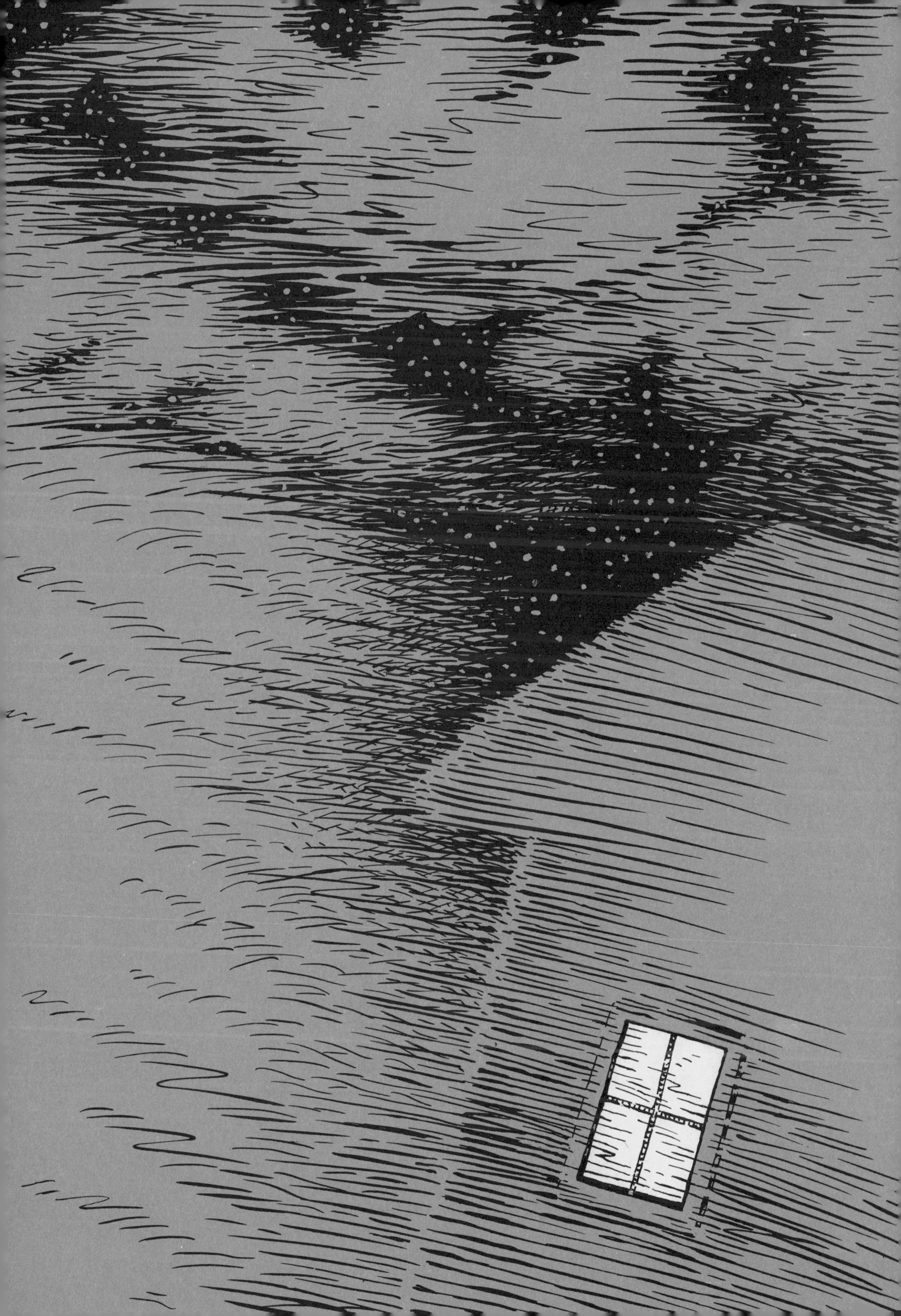

Good night.

THEODOR SEUSS GEISEL, known to his millions of fans as Dr. Seuss, wrote and illustrated forty-four books. He forever changed the face of children's literature in 1937 with his first book, *And to Think That I Saw It on Mulberry Street.* His last, *Oh, the Places You'll Go!,* was on the *New York Times* bestseller list for over two years. He was credited with bringing fun into the process of learning to read after he launched Beginner Books with *The Cat in the Hat* in 1957.

Long considered a national treasure, Dr. Seuss was awarded a Pulitzer Prize Special Citation in 1984. He received virtually every children's book award, including the Laura Ingalls Wilder Medal and three Caldecott Honors for *McElligot's Pool, Bartholomew and the Oobleck,* and *If I Ran the Zoo.* In addition, works based on his original stories have won three Oscars, three Emmys, three Grammys, and a Peabody Award.

Dr. Seuss was born in Springfield, Massachusetts, on March 2, 1904, and died at his home in La Jolla, California, on September 24, 1991.

Books written and illustrated by Dr. Seuss:

AND TO THINK THAT I SAW IT ON MULBERRY STREET
THE 500 HATS OF BARTHOLOMEW CUBBINS
THE SEVEN LADY GODIVAS
THE KING'S STILTS
HORTON HATCHES THE EGG
McELLIGOT'S POOL
THIDWICK THE BIG-HEARTED MOOSE
BARTHOLOMEW AND THE OOBLECK
IF I RAN THE ZOO
SCRAMBLED EGGS SUPER!
HORTON HEARS A WHO!
ON BEYOND ZEBRA!
IF I RAN THE CIRCUS
HOW THE GRINCH STOLE CHRISTMAS!
YERTLE THE TURTLE AND OTHER STORIES
HAPPY BIRTHDAY TO YOU!
THE SNEETCHES AND OTHER STORIES
DR. SEUSS'S SLEEP BOOK
I HAD TROUBLE IN GETTING TO SOLLA SOLLEW
THE CAT IN THE HAT SONGBOOK
I CAN LICK 30 TIGERS TODAY! AND OTHER STORIES
I CAN DRAW IT MYSELF
THE LORAX
DID I EVER TELL YOU HOW LUCKY YOU ARE?
HUNCHES IN BUNCHES
THE BUTTER BATTLE BOOK
YOU'RE ONLY OLD ONCE!
OH, THE PLACES YOU'LL GO!

Beginner Books

THE CAT IN THE HAT
THE CAT IN THE HAT COMES BACK
ONE FISH TWO FISH RED FISH BLUE FISH
GREEN EGGS AND HAM
HOP ON POP
DR. SEUSS'S ABC
FOX IN SOCKS
THE FOOT BOOK
MR. BROWN CAN MOO! CAN YOU?
MARVIN K. MOONEY WILL YOU PLEASE GO NOW!
THE SHAPE OF ME AND OTHER STUFF
THERE'S A WOCKET IN MY POCKET!
OH, THE THINKS YOU CAN THINK!
THE CAT'S QUIZZER
I CAN READ WITH MY EYES SHUT!
OH SAY CAN YOU SAY?